PETTICOAT BAY

Tess Summers cannot believe she has been given a month's holiday in Mallorca. Not too happy to find she is sharing the beautiful villa with writer Jackson Luff, Tess resents his know-it-all attitude, though when she learns he is the villa's owner and he did *not* invite her, she is horrified. He persuades her to stay and help discover who did. When Jack's stepbrother and friends sail into the bay bringing Jack's very good friend, Lorna, part of the mystery is solved. Tess decides to leave the island before she makes a fool of herself, but Jack has other ideas...

PETTICOAT BAY

PETTICOAT BAY

by

Joan Emery

Dales Large Print Books
Long Preston, North Yorkshire,
BD23 4ND, England.

British Library Cataloguing in Publication Data.

Emery, Joan
    Petticoat Bay.

    A catalogue record of this book is
    available from the British Library

    ISBN   978-1-84262-574-3 pbk

Dales Large Print is an imprint of Library Magna Books Ltd.

Printed and bound in Great Britain by
T.J. (International) Ltd., Cornwall, PL28 8RW

CHAPTER ONE

Tess Summers opened her front door saying, 'I'm ready – Oh, sorry,' she said to the postman with a broad smile, 'I thought you were someone else.'

'Lucky someone else.' He grinned, offering an envelope and signature pad and pen. 'If you could sign number 6, please, then print your name.'

Back inside Tess looked at the envelope before eagerly tearing it open, curious to know where it came from. She was reading the solicitor's letter a second time when the doorbell rang again.

'Ready?' her friend Kathy said.

Tess waved the letter. 'This just came in the post. I've been given a month in a villa in Majorca especially to do my writing. All expenses paid.'

'You don't believe that do you?' Kathy scoffed. 'I bet you have to phone one of those expensive numbers that cost you a fortune only to find you've won a fifty pence voucher.'

Tess shook her head feeling bemused and a bit bewildered. 'It's from a London firm of solicitors who say their client wishes to remain anonymous but hopes I will accept the gift as a thank you for all my past help. What do you think?' She handed the letter to Kathy. 'It looks and sounds genuine, but I can't think of anyone who might want to give me such an expensive present for something I don't remember doing.'

'You're right, it looks and sounds convincing. And the plane tickets are in your name.' She handed the letter back to Tess, who read it again.

'It's expensive paper and letterhead,' Tess mused still mystified. 'I'll telephone this Miss Dillon they say to contact if I need confirmation. I'll do it now.' She walked over to the phone and dialled the London number, nodding to Kathy as the girl at the other end announced the same name as on the letterhead. 'Could I speak to Miss Dillon, please? This is Teresa Summers speaking.'

Five minutes later both girls were sitting down with grins all over their faces. 'Wow, lucky you, a whole month in Majorca.'

'And not a penny to pay – everything included.' Tess laughed out loud. 'Oh, Kathy, I can't believe it,' she said. 'But who on earth can have given me such a super present?'

'What about your aunt? You have no other family have you?'

'No, there is only Aunt Teresa, and John, of course,' she said naming her aunt's husband of less than a year. They were on an extended late honeymoon visiting his native New Zealand. 'Besides she thinks I'm still running Richard's office.' She screwed her mouth at the thought of her ex-boss, Richard Cole, owner and headmaster of a small private boys' school. 'So being away at the beginning of the school year is definitely out. With Aunt Teresa being a teacher I've never had a September holiday.'

'I know what you mean. I never thought about it until I was teaching, too,' Kathy said. 'But your mystery benefactor must know you quite well.' Tess looked puzzled. 'You keep very quiet about your writing, don't you.'

'That's true, so who knows I've been trying to write? And who would have arranged it for the first day of term – oh!' She slapped her hand to her forehead.

'What?' Who?' Kathy demanded.

'It's got to be Richard.' Her friend's frown cleared as Tess explained, 'Don't you see – he's arranged it for the first day of term so I can't go steaming in to school's first assembly and denounce him for the rat he is.'

'Of course,' agreed Kathy enthusiastically, 'And that's just what he deserves. Huh, trying to say you were only temporary when you'd done his secretarial stuff for a whole year.'

'I did tell him I was entitled to cash in lieu of notice, but he wouldn't admit it. Only said I'd be better doing one job at a time.' She sighed. 'I could understand that if I'd not done everything and more that old Miss whats-her-name used to do.' She humphed, then added, 'Aunt Teresa used to say it wasn't the same happy place since Richard bought the school. I suppose I should have known better than to have gone out with him, but I believed his "benevolent-man-about-town act". And he was very pleasant at first, for all he's a real perfectionist.'

She hadn't known just how much of a perfectionist, nor had she told Kathy why their relationship had finished. He had admired a bikini in a store window and hoped to see her in it. When she confessed to never wearing a bikini because of the many scars on her back from when she was trapped in the train crash that had killed her parents and little brother, Richard became a cold stranger and never asked her out again. Shortly after she had been out of a job.

Until then she thought she had won her battle of self-consciousness, but that took her right back to when she'd come to live with Aunt Teresa and some of the girls in her new school taunted her about her scars, seen when they were all in the showers after games. She had been twelve years old.

Kathy pulled a face, 'You never said, but I suspected it was because you wouldn't give him your body that he got rid of you.' Tess laughed as her friend carried on, 'Well, I did hear he's been seen with a little blonde bimbo on his arm and that she is now his personal assistant – with the accent on the personal.'

'Serve him right if she can't type,' Tess said then her eyes twinkled wickedly, 'You know, I think I should send him a postcard from Majorca, just to say thank you.' They both laughed. 'That'll show him what I think of his precious anonymity.' After shredding Richard Cole's character some more, Tess straightened her face and said solemnly, 'Yes, I must accept his kind gift. It's only fair. He would hate to have wasted so much money,' adding, 'It must have cost him a small fortune.' Her face creased in another broad grin. 'And Aunt Teresa will be delighted.'

Their shopping trip forgotten for the moment, they got down to the serious part of what Tess might expect on this free trip to Majorca. Would the villa be near the sea? Would there be a pool? And naturally, the contents of Tess's wardrobe and drawers had to be examined before they went shopping.

Tess stared in amazement. She'd expected the villa to be a small holiday place crowded in among other small villas. But now, stepping from the taxi, she rummaged in her flight bag for the address, sure this was the wrong place.

The driver, expecting his money, frowned to see the same piece of paper he had seen at the airport. Tess pointed to the address, shaking her head saying, 'No, no,' while she searched frantically in her head for the Spanish for wrong house.

Perplexed, the driver nodded, 'Si, si,' he said, pointing to the paper then the house. His face lightened at her obvious surprise, 'Es muy grande, si,' he said before pointedly looking in the cab at his meter and quoting the fare. Tess paid him, then stood watching the car disappear down the drive.

There must be a mistake – there was no way Richard Cole would hire this place for her.

Oh, Lord, suppose he'd just bought the plane ticket and put this address to make it look authentic? Surely, not even Richard... She didn't know what she was thinking for the minute and stood beside her soft roll grip collecting herself.

There was nothing to be achieved by dithering; but before she knocked and in case she was shown the gate, she would just have a little look... She'd caught a glimpse of a spectacular view as the taxi swept round the drive – heavenly blue sea over the tops of trees – yes, there it was.

Feeling a bit like Goldilocks, she went

farther round and was not disappointed. A wide expanse of patio with a low ornamental wall housed a long, solid wood table shaded by a large, attractive sun umbrella. The table's six arm chairs were cushioned in pale green chintz with cream and grey-blue roses to match the umbrella. Very smart.

Tess found herself looking over the wall down on to a temptingly cool, green swimming pool which made her aware she was hot and sticky with the sun beating down on her unprotected head.

Now, if she really was Goldilocks she would strip off at this point and take full advantage of the deserted looking villa and dip in that inviting pool.

Well, you're not Goldilocks, she reminded herself, and hurried back to the front picking up her bag on the way. As she went she heard a car engine going away in the direction of the gates. Oh, dash, she'd missed whoever was in and she might have got a lift to the nearest town, or at least some information.

With no sign of life at the rear and the car

driving off, it was unlikely anyone was in, but while she was here she might as well knock and see.

Hefting her bag she walked up the shallow steps to pull the well-used bell knob.

Almost before she heard the clang through the huge, shiny black door, it swung open.

A tall, good looking man with red-blond hair appeared none too pleased to see her from the ferocious scowl on his face. And before she could speak he ground out, 'And you are?' He didn't wait for her to open her mouth. 'One of my brother's little jokes?'

She saw his expression alter slightly as she just stood there shaking her head and holding up the envelope she had received from the London solicitors.

Then she remembered who she was – a grown woman of nearly twenty-four and she wasn't about to allow anyone to intimidate her.

If the episode with Richard had taught her nothing else, it had taught her that there were the walkers over and the walked on, and she definitely was not going to be walked on. Who ever tried it had better watch out and right now that meant old tawny head here.

She had already snapped her mouth shut and taken the hand back with the envelope as she pulled herself up to her full five feet six inches, green eyes flashing with her own fury.

'I don't know what that's supposed to mean,' she positively snarled, then drew breath, aware that her heart was sledge-hammering in her chest. But she felt like hitting him with her roll bag when she saw his eyes shining and beginning to crinkle at the corners.

She almost hopped up and down in fury; how dare he think this was funny? The ... the ... moron. 'The taxi driver obviously got it wrong.' She swung round on her heel and walked down the steps, ignoring his,

'Hey, wait.'

Let him shout after her, she wasn't stopping, and besides, tears of anger were streaming down her cheeks and she wouldn't give him the satisfaction of seeing her cry.

'I didn't mean to upset you,' he said moving round in front of her and walking backwards so he could see her face. She turned it away from him.

'You haven't,' she snapped and carried on walking round him as he stopped in her path. He leaped ahead to stop her and when that failed, grabbed her arms.

She stood stock still, quivering with rage, 'Unhand me.' Her tones were icy as she looked him in the eye.

His exploding laughter threw her completely and before she knew it they were both laughing. 'Oh, dear,' Tess said weakly, not sure where to go from there.

'I believe the line is, "unhand me, foul knave". But shall we start from a proper beginning?' He had sobered rapidly, except for those eyes, she noticed, and thrust out her hand.

'Tess, short for Teresa, Summers. How do you do?'

'Jack, short for Jackson, Luff. How do you do?' he countered, shaking her hand. 'Now we have been formally introduced, ma'am, how may I help you?'

'Don't...,' she began, then straightened her features. 'It did sound rather Victorian, didn't it?' She felt in a bit of a dither, but took the letter from the envelope and held it out. 'I'm trying to find this place.'

'You've found it,' he said baldly, a sweep of his arm indicating the large house behind them, as he went on reading the contents of her letter. It was taking him a long time to read the solicitors' formal notification of her gift of a month's holiday at the villa. When he looked up she took back the letter. He didn't need to know of her connection with Merryhew School and Richard Cole, or her ambition to write books for children.

Disbelief warred with delight as she looked again at the long graceful lines of the well kept, white painted house, its black painted shutters blinding the windows.

'Heavens,' delight won and her face

reflected it. Then a thought occurred, the villa wasn't only for her, it was obviously a Writers' Retreat. She had heard of them back home. 'Are there likely to be many of us here, do you know?'

His expression was unreadable but he was watching her closely as he said, 'There will be no others here for some time. Except Rosina, of course. She's er ... the house-keeper.'

Tess didn't know whether she was pleased, dismayed or what, at the thought of sharing the villa with someone else – particularly this someone else.

'Have you been here before, er, Mr Luff?'

'Many times, er, Miss Summers.' She expected to see the laughter back in his eyes, but he just inclined his head gravely. Impulsively she said,

'Tess. Please call me Tess.'

'Jack.' He allowed himself a polite smile now and shook her hand again, then frowned as he said, 'Come on, I'll show you round.' She noted his frown. He'd thought he had the place to himself. Too bad, Mr Luff. Then she felt mean as he picked up her bag.

In a way it was comforting to know this was a place for writers; she knew these retreats were a way of finding a bit of peace relatively cheaply. As she followed Jack and her bag up the drive she wondered how on earth Richard had heard of it.

'You say you've been here before... Is there a warden or someone I have to report to at the house? I'm afraid the taxi driver didn't stop to ask questions at the gate.' She glanced at him as they walked, noting he carried her heavy bag as if it was feather-weight. He took his time answering – odd if he'd been here many times before.

'Rosina will tell you all you need to know, Tess. But what do you intend to do while you're here? We're a long way from any night life or shops and restaurants.' The polite smile on his lips didn't hide the serious look in his eyes.

Her own smile was a bit guarded as she

told him, 'I don't need any of those things. I'm here to write. What are you here for?' She was pleased that she'd tossed the ball back into his court.

'I've got a final draft to finish and, I don't know about you, but I need absolutely no distractions.'

Ah, that explained a lot and, even as she cast around in her memory for books by Jackson Luff, she promised, 'I won't disturb you, Jack. You won't know I'm here.' He gave her another funny look and she wondered if he knew she could not recall a single thing he'd written.

They walked up the steps and through the open doorway. Tess stopped in the large white and grey marble tiled hall looking about her, her mouth a round o as her breath left her lungs in a deep sigh. 'That staircase could be straight out of an old Hollywood movie,' she said, lovingly taking in the graceful curving sweep with black wrought iron work supporting the polished wood handrail.

He was watching her with interest and she had to work hard not to feel gauche – out of place – to show him that she was used to being among writers and creative people like him. Remember, you are a walker over, she reminded herself. Nevertheless she was relieved to hear him say, 'I'll show you which bedroom you can use, then take you to meet Rosina.' He led the way up the stairs and she followed, keen to see more of this fabulous house.

'My, they keep it in good order,' she observed, glancing through open doors at a couple of beautifully appointed bedrooms as she followed along behind him. 'But, perhaps they're careful who they allow to come here.'

'This is yours,' he said, standing beside the next open door.

She went in. Never had she been in such opulence. The first impression was an all white room with just a touch of gold on the furniture. Then she realised her eyes were wide open and she blinked as she saw his amused face taking in her wonderment.

'Another touch of Hollywood?' he said waving his arm to take in the long white lace curtains at the large bay window and the bed which had been treated to matching lace draped elegantly from a high gold projection above the pillows.

'Am I really allowed to sleep in that?' she asked looking at the multi-frilled white organza covered bed. Even the organza scatter cushions had frill upon frill and Tess didn't know whether to be overawed or amused.

'At least you haven't gone all girlish delight on me.' His approval warmed her and he continued across the room to a door on the far side, saying, 'I'll tell Rosina to change the covers to something more practical.'

Somewhat taken aback by these pro-prietorial sounding words, Tess realised that she had let several such high-handed, bossy statements past her guard, and was stung to remark, 'It's all right, I'll see to it when I meet her.' Then she looked up at him, 'I'll put my things away then go and let her know I've arrived.' Her backward step left him in no doubt that she expected him to get out of her room.

There was his unreadable face again. 'As you please. You'll find her in the kitchen,' he said and went, leaving her feeling a bit guilty for putting on an imperious I-can-manage-thank-you voice. After all he was the old hand and she the new girl.

CHAPTER TWO

Tess shook off the feeling that she should run after him and apologise. It was no good trying to project a new image, then, when it worked, rush round apologising for it. When they met again, as they probably would for meals, she would put things right.

Opening one of the huge mirrored doors which made up one wall of the room, her sense of humour returned; the single silk dress she had brought was hung with due ceremony and she stood back to survey its 'splendid isolation'. She hadn't been going to bother to pack any dresses, but Kathy had said, 'Always take one good dress, just in case,' – insisting you never knew what was round the corner and, just in case she met a handsome millionaire, she would need something special for when he took her out to dinner.

Tess smiled remembering the fun they had had speculating on the villa. A tiny hut with no plumbing was one suggestion and a palatial Moorish residence set in its own private bay another. Kathy wouldn't believe the luxury she'd fallen into.

It was a pity she wasn't with her, they would have had a good time. But she was here to write, not for a holiday.

The rest of her belongings looked lost in so much space, and that was only one wardrobe. How ever many dresses and things would be needed to fill the lot?

The white theme carried on into the bathroom, but the bath, shower, toilet and bidet were heavily flowered with dusky pink roses on a white ground. The walls, carpet and thick Turkish towels were stark white. Even the soap was pure white, the same as the bottles and jars.

'Probably got ass's milk in them,' Tess muttered to herself. She was beginning to get a funny feeling about this place. It was all a bit too … too much.

Back in the bedroom, she noted again the soft, white leather armchairs and even white carnations filling a heavy crystal vase on a glass table in the large bay. Going over to the windows she looked round the white lace, almost expecting to see bars, though not sure why.

Idiot, she chided herself, but the heady scent from the flowers seemed about to overpower her and she whipped round snatching up her shoulder bag and rushed out of the room, shutting the door firmly behind her.

A scream left her lips as something touched her and she turned, terrified, to find a middle-aged Spanish woman looking very concerned. She tried to find words to make Tess understand.

Once Tess realised the situation was of her own making simply because her vivid imagination had got the better of her, she smiled and was treated to a broad smile in return. 'Rosina,' the now happy woman pointed to herself, nodding and smiling as she did so. With a thickly accented, 'All OK?' she happily pointed to Tess's door and Tess nodded and repeated the words, but she was convinced she was going to need her Spanish/English phrase book in spite of Kathy telling her 'they' all speak English nowadays.

'You wan' Senor Whack?' Rosina asked her and her spirits rose, perhaps Rosina spoke English after all. Senor Whack? Perhaps he was the warden. Then a memory that Don Juan, with a J, sounded like Don Whon and her commonsense was sure Rosina meant Jack Luff.

When she asked where she might find Jack, her hopes that the housekeeper could speak English were dashed as the poor woman's frown and shaking head proved her wrong. 'Come,' she instructed, beckoning for Tess to follow her downstairs, then down more stairs behind the 'Hollywood' staircase.

'You wan' Rosina?' she said, proudly indicating a beautiful pale blue tiled kitchen. They passed several more doors, but Rosina kept on going until she came to three steps with a door at the bottom. 'You wan' Senor Whack.' She smiled, well pleased with herself as she ushered Tess down, then satisfied, she turned and returned the way they had come.

There wasn't a lot of room at the bottom of the steps and Tess found herself wondering what to do. Clearly she needed Senor Whack – Jack – to speak to Rosina for her, or at least tell her what the rules were. After all, hadn't he boasted that he'd been here 'many times' before. Well, boasted was a bit strong, but … bother the man. And why did he have to be so good looking? She giggled at her incorrigible imagination…

Suddenly bathed in a shaft of sunlight as the door was snatched open she looked up guiltily.

'What on earth's the matter?' He looked closer. 'You were giggling – I thought you were crying. Well, come in,' he said testily, then added, equally bad temperedly, 'What do you want?'

Feeling like a schoolgirl called into the head's room she followed him in, then forgot how she felt as she saw books and typescript all over the place. A big flat screen and keyboard took pride of place on a large desk to one side of the room; there could be no mistaking this for anything other than a writer's workroom. Then a small leather topped desk in the window drew her attention to the magnificent panoramic view of the tiny bay and beyond.

'How beautiful,' she said, her green eyes shining with pleasure. 'I don't think I'd get any work done if I sat here.' She turned to look at him and found he was watching her with that odd puzzled expression she was beginning to get used to. 'You obviously sorted this out as a perfect spot to work. Lucky you.'

He gave her a wry smile and said, 'Yes, lucky me.' They stood facing each other and Tess thought he was assessing her, weighing her up for some reason. It was a peculiar feeling because he seemed to be disappointed. 'Now, Miss Tess, short for Teresa, Summers, what can I do for you?'

She wanted to tell him about the odd sensation she'd felt in her room, but this light impersonal way of speaking did not encourage confidences. It was completely irrational she knew, but she felt let down – she wanted to be able to tell him things that perhaps others might think strange.

With an effort she straightened her shoulders and smiled, 'I've come to apologise for being frosty to you earlier. You were right, I do need your help.' She looked for a softening in his face and was relieved when she saw it.

'I don't remember telling you that you needed my help,' he said quietly. 'But if you don't speak Spanish, you could have a problem. Rosina does not speak English, except key words such as "you wan"?' and "all OK".' There were those laughing eyes again as he watched hers, now alive with fun as she nodded her agreement.

Tess cursed her guilty flush as his smile vanished and left a blank expression. 'If you could tell me how one goes on in these places...' She gave him a shy smile, before confessing, 'I've never been to a writers' retreat before, though I've heard of them,' she put in quickly as she felt the heat spread over her neck.

There was a flash of disbelief on his face, but it was gone almost before Tess registered it. She must be feeling extra sensitive about things because everything was so new to her.

Jack took her back to the kitchen where a smiling Rosina greeted them and he spoke in rapid Spanish. Definitely not Holiday Spanish. Then they went into a spacious lounge where the soft stuffed furniture matched the colours on the patio, and grey-blue rugs were scattered on the brightly polished woodblock floor.

Tess's face lit with pleasure. 'What a lovely room,' she exclaimed. She wanted nothing more than to kick off her sandals and flop down on one of the large settees with a good book.

'I thought you might prefer to sit outside,' he said. 'Rosina is bringing some fresh lemonade – her own recipe – not the sugar water that passes for lemonade one buys in England.' He stood waiting for her to choose, one eyebrow raised and, he was almost smiling.

'I think it might be as well to go outside. If I sit on one of those,' she nodded to a settee, 'I'm sure I'll fall asleep.' Realising the remark was hardly flattering to her companion she hastily made amends. 'I mean to say ... I think I'm tired after the journey,' she finished limply, her eyes darkening with confusion.

Jack laughed and said, 'Come on, sleepy head, we'll sit outside and keep you awake while you have a drink. Then you can rest.'

A short time ago she had been wishing she belonged here; to sit under this umbrella at this table and be able to swim in the pool she knew to be on the terrace below. It was too good to be true, but she kept her thoughts to herself.

As they sat down Rosina came out carrying a tray with a tall glass jug full of pale lemon liquid and clinking ice. There were glasses and a plate of sweet pastries. Jack offered them to Tess. Taking one, she thanked him, then watched thirstily as he poured the lemonade.

Very much at home, he stretched his long legs in front of him, then touched his glass to hers. 'Salud,' he said. 'May you achieve whatever you set out to do.' Tess's smile faltered as his seemed to hold a bitter quality, almost self-derisory. He was in a funny mood, not saying much, just looking into his glass most of the time. She drank her lemonade slowly, trying not to show the turmoil her tired brain was in.

Later, as she went back to The White Room she reminded herself that she did not really know Jackson Luff so there was no way she should understand him; except for an odd feeling that she'd known him a long time. Perhaps he was tired too, or perhaps this place had a funny effect on him as it seemed to have on her.

Reluctantly she opened the door to her bedroom and went in, this time aware of the white carpet covering the floor in sharp contrast to fresh polished wood and scatter rugs in the other parts of the house. There was a white painted door in the wall opposite the mirrored wardrobes she'd missed before; she would see what delights it might reveal before she rested.

Relief washed over her when she found herself in a little sitting room furnished in cream and blues and brick colours. The polished wood floor shone like the rest of the house and she slumped down on the little sofa. Another door was slightly open and she got up to see where it led.

Not sure whether she felt like Goldilocks again or Alice in Wonderland this time, she pushed the door wider.

An attractive bedroom greeted her eyes and suddenly she was wide awake and opening cupboards and drawers to make sure that no one was occupying this room.

That's it, she told herself five minutes later as she closed The White Room door into the sitting room and carried the last of her things through to her new bedroom. She could have her nap now, although the relief of leaving the other room had exhilarated her, it would be as well to rest. She would just lie down and close her eyes for a while.

'Tess.' Even as she came from the depths of sleep she could hear the exasperated relief in Jackson Luff's voice and opened her eyes to see him walking from the sitting room doorway across to a door, which she assumed opened on to the corridor.

She struggled to sit up in time to hear him calling in Spanish, then he turned and sat on the chair beside the bed looking annoyed.

Tess remembered that she had commandeered this room without so much as mentioning it to anyone, but wondered what it had to do with him. Before she could voice her thoughts he said, 'You do realise you have caused a great deal of trouble? Your thoughtless disappearance put Rosina into a flap.'

A little voice in her head reminded her she was not going to be walked on again and she stood up. At least with him sitting down she didn't have to look up and she found she quite liked that. Moving nearer to him, and pleased that such a tactical move made it difficult for him to stand, she nevertheless apologised, 'I'm sorry, but I had no idea Rosina might want me so soon. I just needed to rest for a few minutes–'

'A few minutes? Good God, woman, you've been asleep for five hours.' He seemed to find pleasure in her gasp of dismay as she looked towards the window and saw it was quite dark outside, then realised lights were on in the room.

'I'm … I'm…'

'Sorry, I know,' this time he spoke wearily, pushing his fingers through his already untidy hair. Neither spoke as they simply looked at each other. 'Shall we go down to dinner? Rosina had it ready half an hour ago,' he said standing up then moving to the door. 'I'll see you downstairs when you're ready. We don't dress up for meals here,' and he went out, not a happy bunny.

Oh dear, she'd obviously kept him from his dinner. She washed quickly and, in spite of being given permission not to, changed her crumpled outfit for a fresh blouse and skirt. The pretty turquoise of the blouse picked up the splashes of the same colour in the white skirt and at the same time did good things to the colour of her eyes. Feeling better already she skipped out of the room ready for anything, well, practically anything, after she'd eaten. She was hungry.

'Did I take the bedroom you wanted for yourself, Jack?' she asked as she came down to the hall and found him waiting to escort her into a good sized, elegant dining room. He looked somewhat taken aback, she thought, watching his face for clues.

There was a hint of amusement as he said,

'No, whatever made you think of that?' That was that theory out the window. Perhaps he had been annoyed solely for Rosina?

She enjoyed his well-mannered care as he held her chair for her to be seated, before taking his own place at the other end of the polished walnut table. The silver place settings and bone china were all in keeping with the gracious ambience of the house; with the exception of The White Room…

'Are you cold?' Jack's astonished tone made her realise that she must have shivered at the thought of that place.

Shaking her head, she said, 'I'm not cold, thank you,' deciding as she spoke, to explain. 'You will probably think I am being fanciful, but I was thinking of the room you first showed me to.'

'Oh?' He was interested now and she saw the bland polite expression change slightly to crease his forehead.

'I suppose I am being silly.' She looked at him again and stopped playing with her knife handle before carrying on. 'But I found all that white ... er ... froth in the bedroom too much for me.' Her eyes had darkened to deep sea-green as her brows drew together. 'It was weird but I felt...' she searched for the right word, 'claustrophobic. I've never felt anything like it before.' She laughed a bit unsteadily. 'But then, I've never been anywhere quite like that before.' She looked straight at him. 'Has it always been like that? I mean, the rest of the house is lovely... The room does look pristine fresh ... so I just wondered...?'

He looked puzzled ... but ... doubting? She thought he was going to say something about the room as Rosina came in with a soup tureen.

He didn't bring the subject up until they were alone again, then Tess was in two minds whether to be relieved or disappointed when he said, 'We will talk about it over coffee, shall we?' What was there to talk about? But, she could only agree and wait.

Jack was a pleasant companion, she decided, talking about the island and comparing it to its neighbours, Menorca and Ibiza, when he knew she had visited the other Balearic Islands.

The tension drained away from her as they chatted and ate Rosina's delicious creamy cold Vichyssoise and the best paella Tess had ever tasted. When he asked her about her writing and discovered she was a fairly raw beginner, he told her stories against himself when he first began. They had been laughing together when she looked at him, suddenly aware that he was like almost two different people. The thought sobered her as her mind did a swift comparison with the sternly polite person she had seen earlier.

'Tess?' His voice was concerned and she put the smile back as she faced him.

'I think you said we should talk over coffee?'

He gave her a quick grin, 'I thought we had been talking.' His glance took in the empty coffee cups, but he stood and came round her end of the table. 'Shall we sit outside for a bit or would you prefer to sit in the lounge?'

She chose to stay inside. Somehow, she felt, he had been putting off the moment and now it was here she did not want to miss seeing his face.

'You were going to tell me about The White Room,' she challenged as soon as they were ensconced in the comfortable, linen-covered easy chairs she had seen earlier.

'I thought you might be able to tell me,' he countered, no longer the relaxed Jack Luff of the past hour or so.

Tess sat upright, frowning. 'What on earth do you mean?'

He didn't say anything, but watched her until her face was flame red. 'Very good,' he drawled. 'Are you sure you shouldn't be trying for the stage? I think you might well be wasting your talents trying to write.'

Now, her face felt as though her blood had drained away, but she couldn't take her eyes from him and wondered how she had ever thought he had laughing eyes. They were cold, gold glitter.

She jumped nervously, but he was only leaning forward in the chair. 'Are you saying my brother is a liar?' he asked conversationally. Heavens, how did his brother come into this? And he had mentioned him before…

'Your brother? I don't think I know your brother.'

'Oh, come on, Tess,' he was impatient now. 'He left a message with Rosina that I could expect a guest.'

'Guest? But–'

'–And, as I understand it, the room is exactly as you ordered. And I have the bills to prove what expensive tastes you have, my dear.' His lips twisted in derision. 'I would say dear brother has gone somewhat over the top from what I saw, but it's a bit rich that you now tell me you don't approve.' He sounded annoyed.

'If I do know your brother, I didn't know he was your brother, if you know what I mean?' He looked about to speak but she didn't give him the chance. 'And I definitely did not have anything to do with that awful place upstairs.'

Was it possible that they had been talking at cross purposes all this while? It made sense of several things if Jackson Luff actually owned this villa. She tried to work out the whole peculiar thing; trying to remember exactly how he had reacted from the moment he'd opened the door to her.

'Do I take it that you have been used, my dear? Has my brother given you this little holiday at *my* villa because he has finished with your services?'

Tess's courage failed her now and her new aggressive feminine image was in rags about her feet. It all fell into place, the whole sorry episode. Richard must be laughing – he'd got rid of her– 'Just one thing, Mr Luff. Did your brother–' he didn't seem to want to say Richard's name and she certainly did not, '–know that you would be here now?' She thought she surprised a look of compassion on his frowning face before he answered.

'Oh, most certainly, that is why you were given the invitation for this time.' He ignored her gasp of dismay. 'I was a bit surprised when you showed me your letter; I would not have expected the family solicitors to have been a party to this. But, knowing my brother, he probably sweet talked one of the young secretaries to do it for him.' He stopped and looked assessingly at her. 'You a secretary?'

Oh, dear, she felt about sixteen and stupid as she nodded. Well, she had been stupid – though she did check with the solicitors and what more could she have done? But she was not a criminal and she sat up again, determined to show him that she may have been naïve, gullible, whatever, but she was no longer. 'Yes, I was, but that is neither here nor there. If you will be so good as to allow me to stay tonight, tomorrow I will make other arrangements,' she finished swiftly.

He spoke then, but there was sympathy in his voice, 'Not good when you know you've been made a fool of, is it?' With a shrug of his shoulders he got up. 'I think you could use that brandy you refused earlier, hmm? I know I could do with another.'

She nodded, feeling drained, though still noticing his powerful shoulders as he went over to a small collection of bottles and glasses on top of a low cupboard and poured two brandies. She knew she should be relieved that the puzzle was solved, but she felt oddly empty. The problem of what to do next could wait until the morning, she would be more capable of dealing with it then.

'To us, Tess,' he toasted and she remembered his earlier toast. She wasn't likely to achieve much for some time. She would have to find another secretarial job as soon as she got home and write in the evenings again. 'You look like a little girl sucking your thumb.' Startled, she looked across at him, then realised she had been holding her thumb nail between her teeth. Aunt Teresa always said it looked as though she was sucking her thumb.

Putting the brandy balloon to her mouth saved her from commenting, but the mouthful of brandy was a mistake. Tears streamed down her face as she coughed and spluttered. The glass was taken from her hand and a soft white handkerchief replaced it.

When she had mopped up and got her breath back she thanked him and saw he was holding the glass out. 'Want to chance it?' His smiling face cheered her and she even noticed one thick red-gold eyebrow was raised.

There was relief as she nodded, 'I'll sip what's left and then go to bed.' She felt awkward, very aware of being an unwelcome guest thrust on this man. And yet...

'When I arrived, why didn't you tell me straight away that I'd got it wrong?' It was out before she could stop herself.

CHAPTER THREE

'I told you – I was expecting you.'

Tess stared. 'How? What do you mean?' she demanded.

'I mean that Rosina had a phone call to say you were arriving and Juan, her husband, told me when he picked me up at the airport. If we had had precise details, Juan would have met you, too.' He pulled a matter of fact face and his shrug was almost continental. 'But you managed all right by yourself. Juan's father lives in the gate house and he told us you had arrived.' She watched his eyebrows rise, 'Almost as good as jungle drums, hmm?'

'I expect your brother didn't know that you wanted peace and quiet to finish your book,' Tess suggested tentatively, still baffled that Richard could have a brother so unlike him, or a brother at all. Her forehead furrowed as she recalled Aunt Teresa once saying that the Head was typical of a spoilt only child; he had missed out on the rough and tumble of brothers and sisters and that it was a great pity.

'I'm afraid you don't know my brother very well if you think that would stop his silly practical jokes.'

'Richard? Practical jokes?' Her choked off laugh surprised him she could see. 'I must say Richard is the very last per–'

'Who did you say?' The staccato words stopped her and she saw the fine hazel eyes narrow as he asked again, more controlled. 'What name did you say? Richard? Why do you call Edward – Richard?'

Heavens, was nothing straight forward? 'I've never heard him called anything other than Richard. Richard Cole.'

Jack shook his head, then raked his fingers through his hair. He was obviously as confused as she was. 'Let's sit down and try to piece this jig-saw together.' Tess sat down again, not aware of either of them standing up.

'Who is Richard Cole? Do you know him well?' Jack asked from his new seat on the end of the sofa nearest her chair.

'He's the Headmaster of Merryhew School. I was his secretary until August.'

'And you thought he had given you a month's holiday in my villa?' Those eyebrows were raised heavenward now.

Tess squirmed, feeling thoroughly stupid, but defended, 'He was the only person I could think of who could have arranged it – particularly after the solicitors confirmed that the donor insisted on remaining anonymous. He's great on secrecy.' Her bitter tones told her listener a great deal.

'Is he married?' he asked sympathetically.

'No, he is not,' she snapped, she didn't want his sympathy. 'And, before you ask, neither am I.'

'I'm sorry, Tess,' he soothed and she looked up to see he was genuinely sorry for causing her distress.

She waved a hand to show she understood, then took a deep breath before saying, 'But I still don't know your brother Edward. In fact, I don't know anyone called Edward.' She stopped. 'Except,' a shadow of a smile broke the smooth planes of her face as she paused again, 'Except the Queen's youngest son?'

'All right,' a ghost of his sense of humour acknowledged. 'But we haven't solved our jigsaw – some bits are still missing.' He leaned forward resting his elbows on his knees looking thoroughly relaxed. 'Let's work out what we do have.'

Tess sat back on the plump cushions as Jack began to list the facts. 'My brother, who, incidentally, is my stepbrother, no blood relation, has a weird and wonderful idea of what is funny. We rarely agree.' She saw from his face that this was not the first time he had been Edward's target and, remembering that room again, she could agree with him, his brother's idea of a joke was weird – and expensive! 'And he did know that I had a deadline to meet. In fact, he was very put out when I vetoed a visit from him and his friends; they're cruising the Balearics in a couple of weeks.' He gave her a wry smile. 'I rather think you have been used to get at me.' Her gasp of dismay twisted his smile. 'Don't let it worry you, I won't hold it against you. But, I'm not sure how he fell on you, unless you know someone who knows Edward?'

'I'm almost sure I don't,' she said, thinking hard to make a connection.

'Where did you say you live?' Suddenly he was sitting up as though he had remembered something from their exchange of small talk at the table.

'Near Winchester, why?'

'Ha, that might be the link. I seem to remember that Mary, Edward's mother was living there before she married Dad. And Edward went to school there, but I don't know which school.' He looked pleased and said, 'I'm still not sure where or how you come into this, but I wouldn't mind betting that Edward's devious little mind has figured some tie.' He smiled a lovely smile and, tired though she was, she was ready to melt. 'Right now, young Tess, I suggest we call it a day. And what a day.'

He pulled her up beside him and she felt the hectic tell tale colour rising in her cheeks as he smiled down at her. She didn't know she reminded him of a startled fawn before he turned her towards the door and said, 'Goodnight.'

Oh, she felt wonderful. She couldn't remember when she had slept so well. Lazily she turned over to look at her little travel clock and shot up when it told her it was gone ten o'clock. Goodness, what would Jack – and Rosina – think?

She went into her pretty pink and grey bathroom to shower, amazed that she hadn't given it a thought yesterday, just accepted there would be a bathroom attached to her new bedroom. Heavens, Tess Summers, you easily accept the ways of the rich, she derided herself. She was enjoying her own light-hearted frivolity as she whisked into the bedroom to pull on a pair of baby blue cotton knit shorts and matching T-shirt, happy that they would not look out of place in the glorious sunshine.

Her plait was damp, although she had fastened it on top of her head, so she decided to leave her hair loose after it had had a good brushing. A little moisturiser on her face and neck and she was ready for anything.

Anything, that was, except the nasty thought which stole up on her when she sat on the terrace at Rosina's bidding.

Jack said he had vetoed visitors while he was working, yet here she was awaiting breakfast as though she was an invited guest with every right to be here. In reality she should have been up early making arrangements to go home. What a mess. Perhaps Rosina would know of a cheap place she could afford for a week or two. Or better, she could try Tourist information. They would be used to dealing with problems of finding cheap accommodation – she hoped. It would be a sin to waste the air fare.

Rosina arrived full of smiles as usual, her tray laden with fresh fruit, fruit juice and rolls and butter with peach jam.

After she had eaten she would go and ask Jack if he would interpret for her. No, that wouldn't do. He didn't want to be disturbed and he might think she was trying to wangle an invitation. She certainly did not want that. Her Speak Spanish book was bound to have the phrases she needed.

The sunshine did not seem quite so bright, nor her breakfast as tempting, and she was already on her feet to go and see Rosina when Jack came on to the patio carrying a coffee pot.

'Ah, how's that for timing?' He waved the pot over a cup. 'Ready for coffee?'

'Yes, please,' she tried to sound like a grateful guest, but the flatness was audible.

'Mmm, thought you looked a bit glum.' He looked directly into her eyes. 'Anything I can help with?'

She shook her head. With his voice so sincere and those gorgeous hazel eyes and tawny hair, she was in real danger of making a fool of herself.

He sat down then reached over and took a roll, carefully buttering it before putting jam on one bit. He ate the piece with the jam. Concentrating on jamming and eating, Tess thought he had forgotten she was there, until one small piece remained, then his long, thick lashes swept up and he smiled into her eyes as he held it to her lips.

Automatically she opened her mouth and slowly he put it in, taking so long to remove his finger that her teeth came down on it. His laughing eyes told her it was intentional and she drew back, not quite sure how she wanted to react. She knew she should go, and go quickly, put as much distance as she could between herself and this accomplished tease before her self control was in shreds.

'Jack,' she began before he stopped her, holding up one hand and looking contrite.

'This time I am sorry, Tess. I really shouldn't tease you, but you do blush so beautifully, and easily,' he added with such satisfaction that she knew any flush still on her cheeks was because she was annoyed, with him as well as herself.

She sat up straight and kept her face equally straight as she ignored his words and said, 'I was coming to look for you. I need help to talk to Rosina.' As she explained what she wanted, the smile vanished from his eyes and it was only when she had finished Tess recalled the reason she had been going to struggle with the phrase book and Rosina.

Almost as she had predicted, he said, 'Why can't you stay here?' The frown on his face was familiar now and he carried on, 'There's plenty of room and,' he saw her expression. 'I promise not to tease. In fact, you won't see me, I really do have a deadline to meet.'

She was sorely tempted. Surely she could keep one overgrown little boy at arm's length for a week or two, should he step out of line. After all, Rosina and Juan were in the house. And she did have her own writing...

'I–' she began doubtfully.

'–I promise to behave,' he chipped in, and she continued as though he had not spoken.

'–don't think–'

'–I know what I said, but you won't inconvenience me, really.' He saw her further doubt and his smile confirmed the little boy theory – he thought he'd talked her round. He had! If he stepped out of line, she would leave.

You are a fool, Tess Summers. It would be sensible to leave now. She would say, no, thank you, and pack her things.

So how was it possible that she heard her own voice saying, 'That is very kind of you, Jack. I'll make sure I don't disturb you.'

His handsome face twisted into an odd little grimace as he said, 'Too late, my dear, but don't let it bother you.' And it was in something like a state of confusion she found herself going back to her room.

Determined to get down to her writing, she went into the sitting room between her bedroom and the white room. Now she understood the situation a bit better she could think rationally. The atmosphere in the sitting room was gracious and peaceful, with its muted blues and terracotta on cream. Perfect for her to write, she decided, even down to a small desk set against one wall. She brought her books and pads and pencils through from the bedroom then placed a chair, which obviously matched the desk, in front of it.

Deciding work could wait a few more minutes she opened the long French window and stepped on to the small balcony. If she had ordered the setting it would have looked exactly like this. The sea was the glorious green-blue, typical of deep water with the sun shining unhindered. Then, as little waves broke away and ran towards the golden, near-complete circle of the bay, the colour changed to a soft green before disappearing into the sand to make way for the next gentle onslaught.

Pine trees formed a sloping green canopy giving a clue to the steepness of the fall down to the beach. Tess looked round to see how many other villas shared this delightful little bay, but, unless they were hidden by the trees, there was none.

A couple of hours of work, then a swim in the sea. And if there were no other villas, she might use her new bikini next time. Jack had said he was likely to be shut away in his study, so she might be able to indulge her own private fantasy; swim and lounge on the beach in a little piece of nonsense, the same as other young girls had done while she always wore a one piece swimsuit. Bliss, she thought, and tried to quell a quiver of excitement, but work first.

And hard work it is, she decided, stretching her back just as there was a light knock on the corridor door. Jack? She whisked over to open it to find smiling Rosina with a tray again.

'Ah, Rosina,' and she took the older

woman's arm and drew her over to the balcony, scouring her memory for house in Spanish.

Feeling very satisfied when Rosina went on her smiling way after shaking her head and stating, 'Una, una,' and pointing to the floor beneath her feet, Tess sat down to pour her afternoon tea and eat some of the dainty sandwiches. She was quite peckish now she had time to think and might eat one of the pastries as well.

She indulged in a smug little grin. She had actually made herself understood without recourse to the book or Jack Luff.

Excitement bubbled as she flip-flopped her way down the zig-zag path Rosina had pointed out earlier. It was cool and quiet under the trees, not that there was any real noise near the house, but here the birds seemed to have stopped singing and only the occasional chirrup could be heard. Tess could hardly believe she was going to expose her body to the sun on a beach after so many years. It was twelve years ago since the train accident had trapped her from waist to thigh, leaving her scarred; but worse, had robbed her of her parents and younger brother.

She fought her thoughts back to the present, remembering Aunt Teresa had told her that the best memorial she could give them was to live a full and happy life.

Out of the trees at last she flung off the oversized T-shirt and flip flops and exulted in the hot, pale gold sand as her feet sank into the caster sugar surface. She was about to skip down to the water when she saw something white farther along the beach. Investigation showed it to be a small towel half covered with the soft sand. Obviously been forgotten sometime she surmised, while scanning the bay for intruders. It was exclusively hers, and she ran gleefully into the warm waters of the Mediterranean.

When she'd swum back and forth across the little bay a couple of times she acknowledged that she was not as fit as she might be and had just turned beachward when a sleek head appeared beside her. 'Oh,' she spluttered, thankfully finding she could stand up, just, and turned to give the grinning Jack Luff a piece of her mind.

He stood there taking it, wide bronze shoulders and chest radiating good health. There was the now familiar twinkle in those captivating eyes she saw, so she did not quite believe him when she finally ran out of steam and he said, 'I'm sorry, Tess, but I honestly thought you'd seen me when I swam back into the bay and you were giving me a race for the shore.' He did look suitably penitent, but she had to have the last word.

'You nearly frightened me to death.' She swam away into deeper water; there was no way she was going to walk up the beach with him.

When she turned to swim back she realised she was enjoying watching him. The long straight back, broad shoulders, narrow hips... She didn't know whether to laugh scorn over herself, or look away, or keep watching. She looked away, in case he turned and caught her. With a grimace she admitted a desire to go on watching – he looked so good. If only...

She turned again and as he was disappearing into the trees, he looked over his shoulder and waved and to her everlasting shame she automatically waved back. Chump, she castigated herself, now he thought she'd been watching, when she hadn't really ... well... Slowly she made her way to the beach to retrieve her shirt and even more slowly went up to the house, not wanting to catch up with her host. Dinner time would be soon enough.

Glorious! Standing under the shower threading her fingers through her newly released thick plait and ridding it of all the salt felt wonderful. Unbidden, the picture of Jack Luff came into her head. It had been sheer chance that he had not walked out of the water behind her. She could not bear the thought of him seeing her all too obvious scars, clearly displayed when she wore her bikini. There was a sense of loss deep within her now she felt she must deny herself the pleasure of wearing two tiny scraps of material that passed for swimwear. But she would not risk meeting Jack again on the beach. An old yearning returned, fiercer than ever now she had tasted that freedom. It must be wonderful, swim and sunbathe wearing next to nothing but her hair.

Her sense of the ridiculous took over and she pulled her loose hair over her shoulders to see what it covered. Not enough. She was no Lady Godiver, that was for sure and she tipped the shampoo over her head still wrapped in her thoughts. 'Idiot!' she said out loud and adjured her silly self to get on, get dressed and get down for dinner.

The buoyant mood lasted until she arrived in the hall and heard Jack call from the lounge. Her face suddenly flamed at the thought of seeing him again – those broad tanned shoulders filling his shirt. She stopped her thoughts right there, took a deep breath and went in with a smile on her face. Why she hadn't left her hair loose, heaven only knew. Of course, she felt more soignée with it caught up in a knot on top of her head, but loose it would have helped cover her face.

'Sherry?' he asked from his position beside the drinks tray, guessing 'Fino?' when she accepted. He poured two and came over, giving her one of the crystal cut glasses, then sat down in the chair farthest from her seat on the sofa. He raised his glass to her, 'Salud! Your good health.'

Tess raised her glass and smiled, repeating the toast before sipping the pale gold liquid. She was racking her brains to come up with a topic of conversation that would not remind him of the beach.

'How did...?'

'Did you...?'

They laughed as their voices meshed and she said, 'You first.'

'No, you first, I insist,' and he bent forward expectantly but still grinning.

'It was nothing of world shattering importance,' she complained. 'I was only going to ask how your work had gone today.'

He nodded his head sagely, 'True, not world shattering, but it is kind of you to ask.' Tess waited, watching differing expressions come and go on his handsome face.

'Well?' she queried.

'Yes,' his earnest voice replied.

Looking thoroughly put out, she demanded, 'Yes, what?'

A feeling of relief sparkled through her when his eyes creased, 'Yes, I am well, thank you,' and he grinned, then sobered immediately. 'Oh, dear, Tess, I do believe I said I wouldn't tease you again.'

'That's right. You did,' she confirmed, affecting a put out expression as she sat demurely and waited.

CHAPTER FOUR

Oh, Lord. Tess suddenly realised that she was flirting with Jack Luff. That was the last thing she should be doing and she turned away to hide her dismay, and alarm. What would he think of his uninvited guest? How did she get out of this? She'd never been in this situation before but bravely she turned a pleasant, though dull, smile towards Jack. Just as well. There was a regretful air about him and she tugged at her lower lip with her teeth wondering, what now?

Rosina came into the room to say she was serving dinner and Tess was released from the caprice of her own stupid imagination and gratefully followed the Spanish woman. Outside the room she looked back to Jack and said, 'I'm sorry,' then touched Rosina's arm to get her attention. With gestures, Tess made her understand that she did not feel well and was going to her room.

Thoroughly fed up she dragged herself mechanically through her bedtime routine. Habits can be comforting she acknowledged as she began giving her hair its usual hundred strokes with the brush.

Head forward, she was brushing the underneath hair when there was a knock on the door. 'Adelante,' she called, raising a flushed face to greet the housekeeper. Horror struck, she watched Jack Luff come in as invited. His remorseful expression told her he knew the invitation was not meant for him and they stood in silence for several seconds.

'Thank you for bringing me a tray. It was kind of you.'

'Phew,' he said putting the food down on the bedside table. 'I thought the brush was going to be thrown at my head for trespassing.' His cheeky grin made her smile and the tension began to fall away from her shoulders and neck muscles. She realised he didn't miss much as he offered, 'I'm very good at the massage, if you feel the need?'

Her rapid refusal left her flushing madly. Was she so transparent? She hoped not, or he would know she wanted to accept but feared the consequences – her vivid imagination had run beyond the massaging to the caressing before she'd controlled it.

'Thank you for the tray,' she repeated as he came close, but his hand only squeezed her shoulder gently before he said,

'The tray was Rosina's idea, I met her on the way. Goodnight, sleep well, my dear,' and he was gone before she could reply.

Not knowing how she did feel or how she should feel after all the highs and lows and mini traumas she just knew she was not capable of another thought. Tess got into bed and pulled the sheet over her. She slept the clock round.

It was only as she was going out of the door, refreshed and ready for anything, that she noticed the tray Jack had delivered last night. She returned it to Rosina with exaggerated sign language explaining how she had fallen asleep too soon. Just repeating, 'Gracias,' seemed inadequate and she determined that she would work at getting a reasonable vocabulary before she left Majorca.

Her determination was reinforced when Rosina had once again sent her to await breakfast on the terrace and she desperately wanted to know where Jack was. She was not looking forward to meeting him again, and remembered that yesterday he had brought his coffee to drink with her when she was breakfasting. Rosina arrived and in answer to Tess's, 'Senor Jack?' she shook her head vigorously, smiling broadly, and made writing movements with her hand.

Well, that's a relief, Tess told herself when she was alone again. But was it? Why on earth did she feel so dejected? Surely she hadn't enjoyed those spats with Jack? No, she admitted, but she had enjoyed his company the rest of the time. Part of her stamped on the thoughts of pleasure in his company and those gorgeous laughing eyes and insisted that she was here to WRITE.

Well pleased with herself a few hours later, she walked out on the balcony and was just stretching and flexing her shoulder muscles when her attention was caught by the sun's sparkling reflection on the water in the green tiled pool below. Why not? She deserved a swim; she had worked hard.

Disregarding the new bikini she took out her navy blue one piece and slipped it on, but, she promised she would find the opportunity to use the bikini again... The back view of Jack's golden tanned body walking up the beach popped into her head. Tess quickly jotted down the first new words of Spanish she needed to learn, then smiling happily, grabbed a large pink towel from her bathroom and sped lightly down the stairs.

She'd swum half way down the pool before she was aware she was not alone and her gasp left her coughing and choking as she took in water.

'My god, you don't do things by half, Tess.' Her laughing tormentor helped her to the side, holding her up close to himself. She struggled to get free and wipe her eyes at the same time.

'There was no one here when I looked just now,' she complained, her head twisting up towards her balcony.

'Sorry about that.' He looked suitably chaste as he let her go, but she'd seen that twitching brow even as he carried on, 'You must acquit me of evil desires though; after all, I am in the pool today and yesterday you were swimming in the sea!'

She remembered that the pool and the bay belonged to him and she had no right to either. For the umpteenth time the 'Sorry,' passed between them and he burst into laughter.

'One of these days I will get that word writ large and framed. Hey, why so glum?' he wanted to know. 'This is big enough for both of us, but if you like I'll use the sea as usual if you prefer to have the pool to yourself?'

'No, no, of course, this is big enough for both of us,' she assured him, then began swimming again, up and down the pool, ignoring him for the most part, but smiling when they happened to be turning at the same time.

When she clambered out at last he was still going and Tess fought the cowardly urge to go back to her room. She sat on one of the loungers, conveniently placed in the shade and patted herself dry before lying back. She could feel herself relaxing and was pleased she had made the right decision.

There was absolutely no reason for the quivering nerves in her stomach. Jack was a friendly person, that was all, and she need only be friendly herself. It wasn't as though she'd never had dealings with men before – thought none the likes of Jack Luff.

'Mmm, nice to see a smile, even with the eyes closed.' Eyes wide open Tess sat up, moving away from the voice. 'Hey, it's OK, I'm not going to ravish you.' He sat on his lounger and said seriously, 'You really don't need to fear me, you know. You are my guest and it's not done to seduce one's guest.'

She shot a glance at him. His old twinkle was back, so robbed the words of formality as he stretched out, folding his arms beneath his head and closed his eyes. 'O'course, away from the villa and I wouldn't give much for your chances, beautiful Tess.'

'Hah, in your dreams!' But she rather liked being called beautiful. Hmmph, her struggling, aggressive feminine self nearly threw in the towel at that point, then was horrified as a little chuckle escaped her. Her glance shot towards him once more but to her relief his eyes stayed closed – he hadn't noticed.

'Stop worrying, Tess. Worrying won't make a bit of difference… Hasn't life taught you that yet?' His voice soothed her and she closed her eyes again, but the soft voice went on, 'Now might be a good time to talk.' Green eyes met smiling gold ones.

'Talk?' The word sounded cracked and she swallowed hard. 'I'm not sure I know what you mean, Jack.' Did he know how he made her feel? She sat very still, waiting.

'Put very simply, Tess Summers, you are

turning my world upside down and inside out.' Before she could respond in kind he had sobered completely and said, 'But it cannot be with a deadline to meet.'

'Is that so, Jackson Luff? Well, let me tell you, your … your women may find you irresistible, but, I can take you or leave you – you do nothing for me.' Okay so she lied, but she was so mad with him she actually believed herself.

'It's that word again, Tess,' he said apologetically, 'I am sorry. I've managed to get hold of the wrong end of the stick… No excuse, except, well, – never mind– Put it down to my over active imagination.' He gave her a wry smile. 'One day I might try to count the number of misunderstandings we've had in the short time since we met – I'm sure I'll never believe it.'

He was being so gentle and sweet Tess wanted to tell him he was not wrong, but a cautious voice reminded her, she didn't really know him. And, was she being unwise to stay?

'Please, don't consider leaving,' he half-demanded telepathically. 'You needn't see me at all. I start work at six in the morning and don't leave my study until teatime – but I would be happy to have tea in my room.' The hesitant delivery came with a little smile that said, I will be good if you let me have tea with you. And already Tess was beginning to call herself all kinds of gullible fool.

'Don't be silly. As two responsible adults – well, one and a half – we should be able to conduct ourselves properly at tea. Besides, Rosina will be run off her feet if we're eating all over the house.'

'Does that mean you won't mind dining with me?'

'I won't mind dining with you.' Tess received a lovely smile and her silly heart turned over. Huh, you're a pushover, Tess Summers, the little voice in her head pro-tested. I get tired of telling you – made to be walked on! 'I'll swim in the sea, if you prefer the pool in future...'

'Oh, no,' he stopped her, 'How about if we share? Would you mind using the sea in the mornings and the pool in the afternoon? Or perhaps you would like the sea in the afternoon?' She had a feeling she was being manipulated, but give him his due, he had used the pool today because he thought she might be in the sea. That showed consideration for her feelings and she warmed to him.

'The pool in the afternoon would be fine, thank you,' she said and rose to go, but he was already up and turning to go into the house.

'See you at dinner, Tess,' and he was gone.

She would go for a little walk around the bay, she decided, and picked up her now dry towel and tossed it over her shoulder.

It was very pleasant under the pines sauntering down the path, out of the sun for the time being, enjoying the spicy fresh pine scent.

The beach was different, heat struck up from the baking sand and she retreated into the trees again. She gave up trying to find an easy path along the edge and dropped her towel before running into the sea to cool off.

Lovely. Floating, going nowhere. Even better in her bikini. She stood up – why not? Tomorrow morning – he works in the morning – the bay was hers. Tess walked up the beach very pleased with her decision.

CHAPTER FIVE

'Honestly, Kathy,' Tess wrote, 'I still can't believe my luck. Everything is perfect and nothing to do but write – try to write – but that is going quite well, I'm relieved to say.

I wish you were here. Rosina spoils me – she won't let me do a thing – but I do make my bed and she's given in over that.

I'm getting an all over tan – nearly – I still wear the one piece in the pool, but I have the bay to myself in the morning, so at last I'm using the bikini.

To answer your question, no, I don't see a lot of the owner, we meet at dinner. He is very civil, but preoccupied with his final draft. Doesn't that sound wonderful? Can't wait until I'm doing my final draft.'

Oh, Kathy, I do wish I could tell you about Jack, Tess mentally told her friend, but there is no way I can write down how I feel. Anyway, you would probably think I was an idiot falling for someone when I've only known him for ten days. Truth to tell, I think it was love at first sight.

Tess switched Kathy out of her thoughts; there were some things you didn't make even your closest friend privy to. It was all a bit new and for the last week Tess had been happier than she could ever remember.

It was true, Jack had been very civil, but he was kind and amusing too, and she'd known she was falling more and more under his spell. Watching for his eyes to hold hers with a special look that had her heart singing, became a daily battle within herself. She fought, and fought hard, not to see his warm gold flecked eyes searching her face for signs. She would not let herself believe the instincts that told her he was very interested in her.

Dragging her thoughts back, she finished her letter, then down to the pool, a few lengths, really concentrate on putting some speed on; that should sort her out. Hah! She ignored the self-denigrating voice as she put on her favourite one piece swimsuit. The green matched her eyes her reflection told her before laughing at the vanity of it and twisting her hair into a top knot she pinned it in place. Still smiling to herself she went downstairs and out into the hot sunshine and dived into the cool inviting pool.

Ten hard lengths. That should do, she decided, as she came out of the tumble turn and headed diagonally for the steps at the far end of the pool.

She felt the obstruction buckle as her fingers struck it, but she didn't know what or who until the melee of bodies and thrashing water subsided a bit and she came face to face with Jack. 'Oh, sorry.' Her apology was not convincing – but, dash it, he'd no right to be there!

'I'm sorry, Tess,' he said, treading water beside her. 'I... Shall we get out? I take it you were on your way out?' He still made it a question although they were very near the steps.

Tess swam the rest of the way and was out in double quick time. A cross niggle ran through her as she glanced back and caught the grin on his face. His mouth straightened immediately he saw her looking, but he followed her out and on to the shaded loungers.

'I did ask if you minded me joining you, because I was too beat to walk down to the sea.' There was that appealing little boy look again. She wondered if his future sons would look like that when they were trying to get their own way. Dear Lord, what was she thinking? Jack was still talking… '–you obviously didn't hear me. I did keep to the other side…'

'In other words, Jack, it was entirely my fault for assuming that I had the pool to myself after we made our agreement, and you haven't used it for over a week?' The query was said without inflection; a pleasing effect and she raised her eyebrows haughtily to go with it.

'I did say I was sorry. And it was my flesh

that was gouged – of course – you may have chipped a finger nail. In which case, I am even more sorry, Tess.' The mock penitence jarred her back to full realisation that this pool and these loungers, and her very bed and food were all provided by him. Then the 'gouged flesh' impinged itself on her conscious thought and she found herself looking at three nasty parallel scratches on his side that were leaking watery bloody streaks down his wet body.

He was leaning over to inspect his side, but the scratches were too far round and his twisting was proving unsatisfactory. 'I'll put some antiseptic on them,' Tess said, getting up. 'I have some in my room.'

'No need to go upstairs,' he told her, rising, 'There's a first aid box in the kitchen.' He walked towards the steps up to the house level, but Tess stood still, uncertain, not knowing if he needed her help or not. He turned to look for her, one hand holding his towel over the injury, the other he held out towards her in invitation. She went with him, ignoring his strong outstretched hand.

'I really am sorry, Jack,' she said.

'Have you noticed, our big little word is out of mothballs again?' They went inside. 'Wait here,' he said when they reached the kitchen, 'I'll be right back,' and returned in seconds carrying a small white box with a red cross on the top. 'Sure you don't mind fixing me up? Not afraid of blood or anything?' he checked as he guided her along.

'No,' she stated firmly. 'Haven't you noticed? I'm not afraid of anything.'

'Oh ho, that sounds like fightin' talk to me.' And he grinned back at her as they went down the steps to his study. He held the door open then opened another door which revealed a small but well appointed bathroom. The suite was burgundy and everything else dove grey, very attractive but no one could mistake that it was a masculine preserve. Tess found pleasure in the thought and commented.

'Very handy.' She took the box from him and set about making sure his wounds were well washed and liberally dabbed with anti-septic, then asked if he needed anything else.

'Well, as I've been very brave, I would have thought I could have had a kiss better. But if...' he stopped, using his expressive eyes to full advantage to put her at a disadvantage. 'No? Perhaps you don't want to make me feel better? Perhaps you feel it was all my own fault?' He sighed, raising and lowering his wide shoulders dramatically.

'Jack Luff! I must say that was a superb performance, and, yes, I do think it was your own fault. But I wouldn't like you to think I was less than magnanimous...' and she leaned forward to give him a peck on the cheek.

'Pecks are for sparrows,' he growled, pulling her close and making profit from her surprise softened lips with his own in a tender kiss. Still holding her near he raised his head to look down into her eyes. 'Did you know a man could drown in your soft sea-green eyes?' His husky voice caused a tremor to scurry along the length of her spine and to her finger tips and toes before flooding back to leave a delicious turmoil around her heart.

Words wouldn't come to lighten the air that enclosed them and she could only shake her head in wonder before his face came down again. Her lips parted naturally to allow his more freedom and she thrilled as his tongue pierced the intimacy of her mouth. Never had she fantasised such feelings that washed over her now, and her fingers were touching his face, his neck and in his hair to hold his head closer.

Jack groaned, moving away a little but still holding her as they heard the rattle of china and a knock as Rosina came in with the inevitable tray and her broad smile. She put their tea tray down on the tooled leather desk and left them.

Tess told herself she was grateful for the interruption when Jack offered her the swivel armchair by the desk and said, 'I'll be mum and pour.' She really wasn't sure what the end would have been had Rosina not arrived when she did, and decided to concentrate on Jack's light hearted conversation. If that was what it was; she hadn't heard a word.

Her eyes found his watching her and her heart, that uncontrollable organ, began flipping over again. She smiled, trying to match his loving, tender look.

'Don't be nervous.' The gently spoken words had the very blood in her veins zinging round her body, her tongue moistening her now dry lips...

'Nervous? I'm not nervous,' she told him nervously.

His soft sympathetic laugh made her love for him swell more. 'A cup of tea, I think.' And he turned to pour the hot amber liquid. As he handed her her cup she realised that they each knew how the other took both tea and coffee without having to ask now. The feeling of intimacy had given her a warm glow on more than one occasion lately and she felt it again as she watched him walk over to the chair in front of his writing desk, taking his cup with him.

A pair of high powered binoculars on the desk caught her attention and she asked, 'Are you a bird watcher?'

'There's no need to sound so surprised, I am a reasonably civilised person with normal hobbies.' His thick eyebrows were raised as he looked at her. She noticed his eyes had a suppressed twinkle, then he lowered the brows and pursed his lips, studying her closely.

'And?' she prompted, not waiting for the next words she could see he was considering.

'I lean on that desk to hold the glasses steady.' Tess wasn't satisfied that that was what he had been going to say, nevertheless she picked the glasses up.

'They are a weight, aren't they?'

'They're an old pair, but very good and very powerful. Here, let me show you.' He pushed his chair across the room, but instead of sitting on it as she expected he swung her round in her chair so she was facing out of the window, then he reached over her shoulder taking the binoculars. With his face beside her own he searched for something worthwhile to show her. 'There you are.' He moved his head back while keeping the glasses steady in one hand and pulling her head so she could see what he was looking at.

Tess squinted through the lenses, trying to see whatever it was she was supposed to be seeing as he told her, 'Small bird, light earthy colour. Can you see him on the branch?' he encouraged. 'His wings and tail are a darker shade.' She nodded, quite excited now she had found the bird. 'Olivaceous Warbler – big name for such a little fellow, but he's got quite a voice to make up.'

'Oh, he's gone,' she said turning the glasses away from the trees where the bird had been perched and looking at different things. 'You are right, they are powerful. I should think you can see a long way out to sea if you needed to. Goodness, you can actually see the beach through that little gap in the trees.'

'Yes, they come in handy for repelling boarders and spotting the odd mermaid.' She glanced at him, smiling to share his fun, but his face was serious and he was watching her as he had earlier.

She tried again, 'Do you see many mermaids?' then chuckled at her own imaginings. 'I might believe it if you said you did, in this little piece of paradise.'

'There is a legend,' he began slowly and she looked hard at him anticipating his eyes would be full of merriment; they weren't, and he was carrying on, 'about a beautiful young mermaid who fell in love with the little bay. It may be because it resembled the petticoat it's named for – you did know that Cala Saya means Petticoat Cove, didn't you? – that she was attracted to the golden edged frill round the green sea. Anyway, she desperately wanted to come ashore and walk on the golden sand and under the shady trees, but she dare not leave the water. She couldn't leave the bay either and one day a man came to live in the bay.'

'A handsome, young man, I hope,' Tess chipped in.

'That I can't tell you,' he told her with a straight face. 'He was a strong swimmer, though, and swam every day. He didn't know that the young mermaid always followed him, until the day he was struck by a vile attack of cramp–'

'Pshaw! How unromantic of him.'

'Shut up and listen to the story. As you're not enjoying it I will cut it short and just give you the bare bones.'

'I didn't meant to spoil it. Tell me properly,' she pleaded.

'OK, but don't interrupt again.' She knew it was all light hearted fun and carried on with her role of listening to a fairy story. Suitably contrite she caught hold of his hands with her own and gave a gentle squeeze as he went on, 'The mermaid saved him when he looked like drowning and managed to get him up on the beach on a big wave.

It was some days before the man swam again, but he half knew that a mermaid had saved his life.' Tess was desperate to ask how he half knew anything, but held her tongue, a wide eyed innocent expression on her face. 'Then he saw her in the shallows one day, combing her beautiful hair–'

'Golden hair. Mermaids always have golden hair.' She looked up guiltily and he laughed into her eyes.

'Tess, you are beautiful.' And she loved it when he kissed the tip of her nose, knowing she'd been forgiven for stopping the story again. 'No, this mermaid had lovely brown hair,' he assured her, 'not unlike yours, I should think. Well, after that, they swam together and played in the water every day. And when the young man heard how the mermaid longed to go along the gold sand and under the shady trees, of course, he said he would carry her.' Jack stopped for effect, watching his audience, but she was very good, and just waited, an expectant smile on her face.

'They fell in love, naturally, and the young man finally carried the beautiful mermaid back into the sea, but he didn't want to be parted from her ever again.

The legend goes that when a young man falls in love with a mermaid, if he looks deep into her soft sea-green eyes he drowns with love and they can live happily ever after. And they did.'

'Is that why you like to swim in the bay every day? Are you looking for a mermaid?' she teased gently.

'No, I have already found my mermaid and drowned in her bewitching soft sea-green eyes.'

Tess felt her eyes fill, 'What a lovely thing to say.' She was taken in his arms as he stood them both up and held her tenderly, but very close. They kissed as she hadn't known kissing could be – beautiful. He moved them apart and disappointment came with reality when he insisted they could both do with another cup of Rosina's tea.

It's odd, Tess thought a few days later as she enjoyed her leisurely morning swim, she would have expected to be put off getting down to work now she was fairly sure Jack was genuinely attracted to her – as much as she was attracted to him, but it seemed to have worked in reverse. She was writing as never before – the routine of her early morning swim, breakfast, then writing for hours as one inspired, was almost too good to be true.

Come on, Summers, time to get on with that inspired writing, she chivvied herself, and walked up the beach to the shower Jack had shown her. It was cleverly hidden just inside the trees so it didn't spoil the natural line but was convenient to rinse off the salt.

Towelling herself dry she slipped her outsize shirt on and a pair of briefs and she was ready for the day. Kathy would hardly believe this casual, casual Tess. She was definitely meant to be one of life's lotus eaters – a writing lotus eater, if there was such a thing – and she almost skipped up the winding path to breakfast.

Her happy mood continued as she took her breakfast tray upstairs, trying to guess what Kathy had to say in her letter. Funny, she'd just been thinking about her, though that was probably because she had been expecting to hear.

Reading the letter, Tess could only feel sorry Kathy was busy teaching, and the weather was not living up to its usual golden autumnal late September days. A little grunt escaped her as she buttered another roll while reading the letter beside her plate. She agreed with Kathy, perhaps Richard Cole would find 'perfection' this time and serve him right if he did. Her friend's source of information had told her he was dating the new, very young art teacher at his school. 'In secret, naturally, but I think he gets his kicks that way. I know, I know, you only went out with the man because you were sorry for him. And got trampled on for your trouble! But even you must now realise that you don't help some fool get over his so-called love for you by secret assignations. I remind you advisedly, as your best friend, in case you think of being stupid with the old boy who owns that place! I know you and your kind heart, Tess!

Incidentally, you never did say what age bracket he came into. A full description please, beyond the kindness and the nice smile, so I can visualise your evenings discussing books and plays. Good for you for sticking up for our favourite. I'll bet John Chaucer can knock spots of your stuffy old fellow's writing any day of the week. I'll have to finish writing this – my TV turkey dinner is about ready. I often think of you, not sunning or swimming – eating lovely food somebody else has cooked for you, ENVY, ENVY.' Poor Kathy, she loathed cooking, but loved eating. She would adore it here. And she would like Jack. Tess grinned as she imagined Kathy meeting Jack, especially as she had omitted one or two salient points in her description of him. But enough daydreaming – work.

'How would you like to go out to dinner tonight?' Jack asked as he leaned over to kiss the tip of her nose, his usual afternoon greeting.

'Sounds good to me,' she answered. 'And just in case you fancy taking me dancing afterwards,' she added saucily, 'I do have a dressy dress with me. Thanks to Kathy.'

'Something else I have to thank Kathy for, hmm.' He already knew a lot about her friend from Tess and she explained the 'just in case' theory that Kathy ran her life by. 'You said I should like her and I like her even more.' His eyes were crinkling as he saw her frown. 'No dress – no dance! Now, I get to dance with you and hold you close.'

'Do I take these signs of freedom to mean you have finished it?'

He nodded as he said, 'As near as makes no difference, but I think it's about time I took you out, to see something of the place, even if it is only a restaurant.' He could see she was about to protest, and carried on,

'When I've finally sent if off, if you can spare the time from your own writing–' he looked at her from under his eyebrows, '–I should like to show you my favourite bits of Majorca, and take you to yours.'

'I haven't missed going out, you know. I'm very happy here, but perhaps you feel...' Her concerned expression brought reassurance from him,

'No, my dear, I'm just as happy here. But before we get bogged down in Freudian reasoning of the whys and the wherefores of leaving paradise, I think we should go for a good long swim.' He pulled her to her feet. 'Oh, Tess, you are perfect.'

She saw the tiny frown and knew he had noticed her reaction to his words. She laughed. 'I thought you said a good long swim was needed – race you to the beach.' She sped off with him in pursuit.

Tess put the finishing touches to her eye makeup then looked critically at the rest of her face. She was lucky to have the typical

English peaches and cream complexion that needed only moisturiser while she was here, plus protection from the sun. Kathy always said her skin was perfect…

Jack's remark about perfection had shocked her out of her state of euphoria. She knew she was far from perfect and if that was necessary for Jack to love her, then it would be as well for her to leave now. But, said the little voice in her head, if Jack really loves you he won't mind a few scars. She stifled a cry, then caught sight of the time on her small travel clock and made haste to smooth pink-red lipstick on lips that trembled slightly.

Next, she stepped into her dress, not wanting to spoil her hair, swept on top of her head with a few tendrils falling either side of her face to soften the effect. All ready except for the last bit of zip that she just could not manage – Jack would fasten it for her – then she slipped on the matching green leather strap sandals and that was that. She turned herself about in front of the long mirror and told her reflection she would have to do. Picking up her small purse with her lipstick and hankie inside, she went down to wait for Jack.

'Mmm, a prompt lady. A beautiful, prompt lady.' He took her hands, drawing her close then enfolded her in his arms kissing her gently on her newly reddened lips. 'A delicious, beautiful, prompt lady,' he said licking his lips. Tess laughed and using her hankie, scrubbed them. 'Hey,' he protested, 'I was enjoying that.'

CHAPTER SIX

'Would you do my zip, please?'

'Certainly.'

'Jack!' Tess protested as she felt her dress loosen, then heard him chuckle and felt the warmth of his lips on her bare flesh before he zipped her dress to the top.

She rounded on him and saw his mock innocent face, 'You didn't say what you wanted doing, so I thought the choice was mine.' He grinned. 'This time I am definitely not sorry. You have a beautiful back – it seems a shame to cover it up.'

A frisson of alarm tightened her chest before reason prevailed reminding her the scars were concealed beneath her silk teddy and she could afford to ignore his remarks. She turned for the door, 'I thought you were taking me out to dinner. I'm starving.'

'So am I.' The depth in his voice sent shivers down her spine and it took all her willpower to continue on her way.

'Very nice,' she approved as she opened the door and saw the low slung sports car, shining brilliant white even in the gathering dark of evening. She allowed herself to be put into the passenger seat feeling cosseted. Then a thought occurred to her, 'It was just as well you didn't know I was coming to Cala Saya; Juan would never have got us both in this, even with next to no luggage.'

She saw his teeth gleam as he smiled at her remark. 'Juan doesn't drive this,' he told her. 'He drives the family car – a big, old Mercedes.'

A cold sensation showered over her as her scalp tensed. She watched him walk round the car then ease his long length into the driver's seat. Perhaps, at last, she was about to hear something of his personal life. But the hearing might hurt when he could talk blithely of 'the family car'.

'It's getting a bit past it now. I'll have to

think about replacing it.' She saw a tiny muscle in his jaw pulling, before he looked at her and smiled. 'It was Grandpa's pride and joy and I hate to think of it going.'

He started the sports car and put it in gear, then drove down the drive and on to the narrow road before he spoke again. 'Did I tell you Gala Saya belonged to my Grandfather, my mother's father.' She shook her head but he was watching the road. 'We used to come for family holidays when we were young; naturally, we all loved it.' From her half-turned position she saw he wasn't smiling now. 'Only my sister, Elaine, and I came after Mother died. I don't think Dad could bear it without her, but Grandpa lived here, so we always spent the Easter and summer holidays with him.'

She was silent, aware that she had nearly made a fool of herself yet again with her rampant imagination. Jack carried on, 'When the old boy died he left it to the pair of us. Elaine and Paul were starting a new business at the time and needed capital, so I bought her half.' Just the purr of the engine and thrum of the tyres filled the car.

'He must have been pleased to leave you such a happy house.' Tess felt the need to fill the space, then wanted to know, 'Does your sister ever visit?'

'She usually brings her lot out for the summer holidays and I try to spend a week with them. You missed them by a couple of weeks.' He glanced at her and added with a grin, 'You wouldn't have mistaken the house for a peaceful writers' retreat then, that I can guarantee. Neither would you have got much writing done!' he added cheerfully.

'You sound as though you enjoy being here with them – what are they? Boys? Girls?

'Two boys with two girls sandwiched in the middle. And yes, I do enjoy it. Adrian is twelve, Marie ten, Netta eight and Robert six. All very neat; but if you knew my sister, there is nothing neat about her. You wouldn't recognise Saya when Elaine is in residence.' Tess could hear from his voice that he didn't mind and obviously liked his sister. She didn't know why but the thought was comforting. Possibly because he didn't sound quite so in tune with his step-brother, and from what little she knew she didn't blame him.

'My goodness, I'll bet there aren't many uncles who remember the ages of their nephews and nieces,' she said admiringly.

'I suppose it's because they are the only ones I have,' but Tess knew that wouldn't make any difference to some men, 'and Elaine and Paul have always been very good to me. Probably because they were older and well married, but they gave me a lot of moral support while I was growing up.'

The little car turned off the road into a space in front of a brightly lit restaurant. 'Oh, I've been here before, for lunch once.' Her delightful exclamation pleased her escort.

'I think you'll find the menu is quite a bit more ambitious in the evening,' Jack told her, before swinging his long legs out of the car and coming round to help her. 'Fernando, the son, has worked in Madrid and Paris and delights in putting on a truly international menu.'

They were taken to a table by a young woman who greeted Jack like an old friend, then chatted to him, at intervals smiling at Tess and nodding knowingly. Jack translated the menu and Tess decided she would have watercress cream soup, then spiced prawns with tomatoes and pilau rice. 'Very nice. I'll have the watercress soup with the stroganoff to follow.' The evening was blissful, Tess was so happy as they enjoyed the delicious food and talked and talked. Though she was not sure why it was different, because their evenings were usually spent in the same way.

'I feel quite special,' she told him as Fernando appeared in the kitchen doorway and raised a glass of wine to them, acknowledging Jack's compliments to the chef for a wonderful meal.

'You are special,' he said softly lifting his glass again and touching hers, 'very special.'

His eyes were soft amber across the candle flame and Tess could look and love the way those long lashes guarded them. 'I think we should go now. I want to dance with you – hold you to my heart, beautiful Tess.' He stood up and held out his hand for hers.

She didn't really notice the short drive to the hotel where they were going to dance under the stars but they arrived as three musicians took their places beside the dance floor. Jack ordered coffee from a waiter, but the trio began a slow sentimental tune, 'Coffee can wait, I need to hold you now,' and Tess found herself in his arms as they moved to the music.

It was heavenly, resting her head against his chest, his arms wrapped around her folding her to him, she could go on all night like this – wonderful. He stopped and moved away and she became aware that the music had stopped as well. Keeping one arm round her, he led her back to their table under the softly illuminated trees.

Their coffee was waiting and Tess happily

accepted a cup. She seemed to be having difficulty focussing and thinking, but she could hear the cicadas making their own music in the branches. She sighed. She was very happy just sitting with Jack, a somnolent peace washing over her.

The music started again, another slow number, and she lifted her hands for him to pull her. 'You've got your drowning sea-green eyes again, mermaid, and I don't think I can be trusted to hold you just yet,' he refused gently, shaking his head sorrowfully.

They watched the floor become crowded again and she pleaded, 'Just one more, then home to bed.' She smiled at him beguilingly and loved it when he groaned quietly and pulled her to her feet.

The slow smooch round the floor pressed close to Jack had her arms around his neck and her fingers playing in his hair. She loved hearing his soft little groans, it made her feel so.o.o nice. She didn't understand why he dragged her arms down to hold her traditionally, but she was sorry when he decided to take her back to her seat before the music was finished.

'I think we should go now, my dear.' She couldn't be sure but she thought he said more, though now they had stopped dancing she was having a terrible time trying to keep her eyes open.

'Did you say something?'

'I think – never mind...' he smiled a little quirky smile, 'Shall we go?' She took his outstretched hand and allowed herself to be guided back to the car.

She felt wonderful. It had been a truly lovely evening and as soon as she could open her eyes she would tell Jack so.

'Come on, Sleeping Beauty. Out you come.'

The car had stopped, she knew that; Jack was picking her up, but her eyelids were too heavy to lift! Mmmm ... she loved the male smell of him and nuzzled closer. A dee ... eep breath ... gorgeous.

'Come on, love, don't go to sleep yet.'

'Sleep?' the sibilant sound pleased her. 'Not yet, Jack. Do you know what I would like?' Her face had a beatific smile and she looked at him with newly focussed – almost black-green eyes.

'No,' he prompted warily.

'You to kiss me, Jack. Really kiss me.'

'Sorry, my love, no can do. Now come along – up we come.' And he pulled her up from her chair, but she refused to move further.

'Why won't you kiss me when I want you to?' Her soft lips a temptation for any man and he wasn't just any man.

'Because, dear heart, when I kiss you I want you wide awake, not so tired your eyes can't keep open for ten seconds at a time.'

Her eyes widened and looked up at him. 'I can keep my eyes open...' Her head fell against his shoulder and her eyes closed. 'Night, night. Thank you for a lovely evening.'

The sun was lasering through a chink in her

curtains as Tess woke, a smile playing on her lips. She felt wonderful. It had been a wonderful evening and … and she was wearing her silk teddy? How was that? Sitting up abruptly, she struggled to remember the end of the evening.

They had gone dancing after their meal; soft lights and sweet music and being held in Jack's arms – yes, yes she remembered that – but she could not remember taking her dress off or even coming to bed at all. Oh, dear. Whatever would Rosina think of her? Incapable of undressing after an evening out. Her Spanish was improving, but it wasn't good enough to explain that she had forgotten a second glass of wine sent her to sleep.

Work, that was what she was here for. She scrambled through her shower and dressed before getting back to 'Rover's Adventures' and the big black dog who was found by a little girl when he had been abandoned.

By lunchtime she admitted that she was not concentrating properly and promised herself a walk after she had eaten. Changing her mind, she went down by the pool. Exercise did not appeal, though the book she'd taken from the shelves in the lounge earlier in the week, did.

Jack was a bit non-committal about John Chaucer's style when she had confessed to being a big fan and thrilled to find a shelf full of his novels behind a sofa in the lounge. She supposed she had gone over the top a little, she thought now as she made her way down to the lower terrace, but she really enjoyed reading about the witty, and sometimes caustic, Detective Daniel Thorn who was the hero in all the books. Last night's revelation explained a lot of little mysteries that she just had not liked to ask about. But she was going to have to take a leaf out of Daniel Thorn's book and probe a little harder if she was to find out what sort of book it was that Jack wrote.

Stretching out on a lounger, she sighed, enjoying the comfort. As she found her page she remembered Jack talking about his sister and her family. That explains the John

Chaucer books; nobody has a shelf full of novels they don't like, so they must belong to Elaine and Paul. She had already been prepared to like the couple when Jack spoke about them, but it was nice to know they had something in common.

What on earth was she thinking? Why should it matter whether she had anything in common with his sister and her husband? She must get things in perspective. A frown creased her forehead. Perhaps she was a little in love with Jack Luff. But what was that to anything? He seemed attracted to her, but it was obvious he was trying hard not to be, otherwise he would have wanted to deepen their relationship.

That does it! She'd been refusing to allow thoughts to turn in that direction since she first woke this morning, but now they flew round her like homing pigeons freshly released from their racing baskets.

A hot tide flooded her cheeks as a part-memory told her she'd asked Jack to make love to her. What had happened? Mentally she took stock of her entire body to find if anything felt different. None of her feminine parts felt different – and surely she would know if something as momentous as … as losing one's virginity, the nasty little voice in her head spelled out to her – at her age too! Her scarred body had always held her back, but then she'd never felt like this before about any of her boy friends. Anyway, Jack was not the type to take advantage of her unconscious state!

Ah, Saint Jack, the little voice sniped. He was simply enjoying a holiday romance with her, that much was obvious from the time he spent with her – many afternoons and every evening, in spite of being very busy finishing his draft. But, he is a man of the world; his world thinks nothing of taking a pretty girl to bed.

Tess would not allow that he was other than kind. So...? She failed to silence the spiteful little voice. So he is a kind man and he accepted you as his guest, albeit un-invited, surely he's entitled to payment…

'Oh, hell!' Her savage expletive startled Jack as he came up from the beach unaware his guest was out of her bed.

'Something wrong?' he asked walking over to her. Thank goodness for the dark glasses, Tess thought, knowing they would reflect his face while disguising her own eyes. There was nothing she could do about the flush she suspected would be spreading up from her socks, if she'd got any on.

'No. It's nothing,' she contradicted, 'I just thought of a mistake in the plot...' She tried to smile a welcome, but watched warily as he sat on the lounger next to her own. She knew he wouldn't question her; they might discuss other people's writing, but never their own.

'You'll work it out,' he said casually, but his eyes took in her now pale face. He got up saying, 'I'll be back in a minute.'

He was back in five with a face like thunder and the tea tray.

As she scrambled to get up and help he told her to sit down and he would do it. She sat, wondering what had upset him. She hadn't seen him look so forbidding for some time, not since they'd sorted out her being here, in fact.

Offering a cup, he squatted in front of her. 'You'll feel better when you've had a cup of tea.' His normal sounding voice surprised her and she ventured,

'And will you feel better when you've had one?'

'What?' His amazement lasted seconds, before he laughed and his eyebrows returned to normal. 'Sorry – whoops, the not-to-be-used-word. Yes, I think I might feel better when I've had a cup.' His smile relaxed her, though she hadn't known she was tense, before he continued, 'Just had a phone call from Edward, telling me he will visit tomorrow.'

'Oh!'

'Yes, oh.' He sat on his lounger, drinking his tea and looking thoughtful. 'He said something interesting – at least it might be interesting.' He put his cup down and Tess waited.

She drank her tea, watching the changing expressions on Jack's face. A little crease between his brows showed his concentration then he looked directly at her. 'He asked me how I was getting on with "the old trout".'

It was Tess's turn to frown as she repeated, '"The old trout"? How peculiar. Did he say what he meant?' She looked expectantly at him and was surprised to see the twinkle in his eyes that showed when he was trying to suppress his sense of humour.

'I rather think he meant you.' He was barely keeping a straight face.

'Me?' Her indignation had Jack's laughter spilling over, but he sobered a bit when she asked, 'Why? What did he say?'

'First of all he asked me how I was enjoying the company he'd arranged for me. And when I told him, very much indeed. He said he'd thought she wouldn't be such a bad old biddy–'

'–Biddy? Trout? And you think he was talking about me?' she exploded. He held up his hands as though expecting attack.

'Steady, steady. Hear what I said before you throw things.' She got off her high horse. She was acting like the lady of the house who'd been insulted when she was only an uninvited guest.

Suitably penitent, she looked her apology with a tight little smile and listened.

'I told him I found her delightful company and we spent many happy hours discussing books and literature and the world in general. He made some remark which I, naturally, had to counter – I told him this old trout was the best thing I'd ever seen in a swimsuit.' His frown returned. 'And that was my biggest mistake, because he said he'd call tomorrow to check it out, and rang off.'

'Oh, dear, and then he'll find you've been lying.' She looked up at Jack's unreadable face. 'Would you like me to stay in my room tomorrow? Or go out for the day?' Her face brightened, 'That's it, I can go to Palma for the day, if Juan could take me to Inca to catch the train?' She felt quite pleased with herself; she could actually do something for Jack.

'Tess Summers, you are priceless.' He was smiling his lovely smile. 'I didn't mean that. And I certainly wasn't lying – you are the best I've ever seen in a swimsuit. You are perfect.' A lump of lead thudded in the pit of her stomach and she countered,

'I'm not perfect, Jack.' Her grave tone and face affected his light heartedness.

'Oh, love, don't be so serious, I know nobody's perfect.' He grinned again, 'Just as well, you'd be difficult to live up to.' He leaned over to kiss the tip of her nose and gently squeezed her shoulder and Tess felt her happiness return.

'I haven't thanked you for a lovely evening last night.' She could not look at him as she continued, 'I'm sorry I was such poor company when we got home.' There, it was said, she felt better.

Jack was watching her face and took her hands in his. 'There's no need to look so guilty, you only fell asleep in the car and I had to carry you in.'

The relief. One day her imagination was going to be the death of her. She pulled herself together, managing to smile at him. Then she said, 'What on earth did Rosina say?'

'Rosina doesn't know.' Her fine eyebrows went skywards. 'Ah, I see what you mean.' How could he? she didn't know herself. 'It was quite a night of firsts. The first time I've had a date fall asleep on me and the first time I've played lady's maid. And, in case you are wondering, I treated you as circumspectly as if I had taken the Hippocratic Oath. Besides … but that, as they say, is another story. You have nothing to be ashamed of, and nothing to worry about. OK? Feeling better?'

She thanked him and told him she was still tired and lay down full length on the lounger, closing her eyes.

She knew now that there was no chance for her. He was a kind man, even if his brother could make him angry at times. She must never let him know that she had been hoping for more than friendship and the very light romance they were enjoying. After all, she knew he was a perfectionist, he'd mentioned it several times, usually in connection with his work. Nevertheless, a perfectionist is a perfectionist, she had learned that much from Richard, and with scars like hers she was far from perfect. Perhaps that was why she was still wearing her teddy this morning. Perhaps the poor man had started to take it off, but covered up the scars so as not to embarrass them both.

The other lounger creaked and she turned over away from Jack's sight in case he noticed the single escaped tear she could do nothing about.

CHAPTER SEVEN

'Jack!' Her surprise was clear as Tess came out of the villa next morning. 'I didn't expect you to drive me to Inca. Are you sure you can spare the time?'

'Good morning, and yes, I can,' he told her cheerfully, opening the door of the low slung white Jaguar and waiting for her to get in before he said, 'I thought it was about time we had a real day out. We've both worked hard and I think we deserve it.'

'You mean you're coming shopping with me in Palma?' She laughed out loud when she saw the horror on his face.

'Shopping? I thought we could do a few touristy things while its fairly quiet.' He closed her door then went round to his own seat.

The Kathy phrase 'he's one handsome

hunk' came to mind as she took in his powerful shoulder muscles evident under the navy, short sleeved knit shirt. There was not a spare ounce of flesh on him and with his shirt tucked into the stone coloured lightweight trousers secured with a navy blue leather belt, it could only please any woman to be seen out with him.

But now it looked as though she might not get the chance to shop for a present for Kathy…

One of the walked on! The sly voice in her head sneered.

'That sounds nice, but I really must use this opportunity to do some shopping, Jack,' she stated, ready to insist he take her to Inca to catch the train if he demurred.

'Compromise? We do your shopping before lunch, then have a wander round the Cathedral and perhaps visit an art gallery or two this afternoon?' She knew that appealing voice and look and as always she melted. After all, she told her jeering self, that is exactly what she would love to do! 'We could take the scenic route home and stop in Soller for dinner. We could even ride the tram down to the harbour if we're not too late.'

'My, such enthusiasm,' she teased. 'I had no idea you were a covert tourist, Jack.'

'If you're not careful Tessa Summers, I shall stop this car and give you the kissing of your life.' She looked at the constant traffic now they were on the main Inca to Palma road and judged she was safe. Anyway she loved the way he'd called her Tessa. She'd been called Tessie, which she disliked, but never Tessa. She knew her thinking was illogical, but she didn't care – today she was going to enjoy!

'Promises, promises,' she provoked, a little smirk on her face which turned to concern as he turned the wheel and there was a squeal of tyres as he shot up a slip road. It went on to a farm lane and he drove into an open gateway before he stopped.

Looking at his stern face, she wondered what lecture he was about to give her. Then he turned, 'Not the best of cars for this, but I like to keep my promises...' undoing his seat belt as he carried on, 'while they're still fresh enough for the recipient to appreciate my good faith.' He leaned over pulling her towards him to kiss her still surprised lips. 'Darn it. Can't keep a promise like that, can I, my love?' and he let her go.

Poor Tess didn't know whether to laugh, or cry with disappointment, even as she registered 'my love', then he was out of the car, opening her door, undoing her seat belt and helping her rapidly out of her seat. With his arm about her he led her to the shelter of an overhanging tree. 'This is better, mmm?'

Tess agreed silently as her heart sang and she gave herself up for the kissing of her life. Suddenly she found herself being thrust away and opened slumberous eyes to find Jack breathing heavily, holding her arms. Bafflement replaced the love-soft look as she waited, not knowing what was expected of her.

He leaned over and hugged her before letting her go. 'Sorry, Tess. I guess this wasn't such a good idea after all. We'd better be on our way, but we'll take the old road, it's more interesting.' He put his arm round her shoulders and turned to the car. His attempt at lightness fell a little heavy, but she was glad he had tried. As they drove off she added her mite,

'If it helps, you did keep your promise, Jack. That was the kissing of my life.' She felt a bit shy saying the words, but was cheered when his hand left the steering wheel and gripped hers for a second.

They talked about the road, the fields they passed, the villages they went through and Jack smiled when Tess mentioned how all the houses, fronting the road in one village, must have children living there. 'How do you figure that?' he asked and was more amused when she pointed out the slats outside the front doors for the guards to stop little ones wandering outside. 'They probably do serve that purpose,' he told her, 'but they are for boards to stop the water coming in. When it rains heavily or when there is a flash flood racing down from the mountains and off the fields.' A glance showed him her astonishment. 'I have been on this road when only lorries could move through the deep flood waters on the flat, but down this steep bit it runs like a river. Vehicles, however careful, cause waves and the people here board up at the first hint of rain in the mountains. Talking of rain, we've been very lucky this last couple of weeks; we can get some quite spectacular thunderstorms at this time of year.'

He gave her a little sideways grin. 'I don't suppose you are scared of thunderstorms, are you?'

'What a funny way to ask,' she reproached. 'I could think you wanted me to be scared.' She watched his face for his reaction.

His wider grin rewarded her vigilance. 'Well, if you were, and we did have a nasty storm, I could comfort you. I'm very good at comforting – you can ask Elaine's younger ones, they say I'm very good at comforting. Mind you, most of my practice has been after falls from bikes and icecream slipping prematurely from its cone.'

The fact that he amused her, she kept to herself. 'Jackson Luff, do you know, you have never told me what sort of books you write?'

'Heavens, how did we get round to that?'

'Your conversation smacks of telling stories to children, that's how we got round to that.' She had stopped watching the road some time ago and was surprised when he stopped the car and pulled on the hand-brake saying,

'Here we are.' And he still hadn't told her about his books, Tess realised in frustration as they left the car to walk along the palm lined Paseo de Sagrera.

'This is lovely, under the trees.' She sighed, stopping to look out across the Bay of Palma, then closer to see the huge variety of shipping hanging on to the marina and harbour as though each was unwilling to let go of its lifeline.

Jack picked up her thoughts, 'What an

assortment. Fishing boats, ferries, cruise liners, yachts–'

'–Oh, you've forgotten your stepbrother is coming to Saya today,' she exclaimed, a horrified frown marring her pretty face.

'No, I haven't.' The statement was so definite that she looked at him, doubt replacing concern that was not wholly quashed when he answered,

'It is not character building to give anyone all they want, you know.' And that was it. He drew her attention to the colourful fishing boats waiting silently in the sunshine for men to take them to sea. Another look at his serious face and she took the hint.

'Look at that monster, there.' She pointed to a huge white and blue luxury craft, standing proud of other smaller ones, moored to a long jetty at right angles to the waterfront. 'Goodness, how do people afford that sort of life style?' As they watched, two young women came to sit on deck, all long blonde hair and bikinis, and Tess was glad she was far enough away to observe without being seen to be looking.

'Ah, here's father with the champers,' she commented as a balding, fat man in a large pair of shorts appeared beside the girls carrying a bottle and glasses. So busy being nosy, she didn't see Jack's unbelieving glance.

'Come on, Pollyanna, we'd better be moving if you want to shop,' and he took her hand as they carried on walking. He squeezed it gently and she relaxed when she saw he'd put his step-brother out of his mind and was his usual even-tempered self again. 'Now this must be one of the best views of any city, anywhere in the world,' he said, stopping a few yards further on.

Following his flamboyant flourish she looked across at the bright stone built Gothic Cathedral standing massively behind the Moorish Almudaina Palace. From where they were standing the view was framed by two tall palm trees. When Tess commented on the building, Jack said, 'And Ramon Llull's statue completes the picture.'

'Yes, it does, but I have no idea who he was.'

'Allow me to inform you,' he said grandly taking her arm while they crossed the road. 'Raimundus Lullus, as he was called in Latin,–' She could see he meant to milk the situation for all he was worth. '–was Majorca's celebrated philosopher-priest who lived in the thirteenth century. Apparently he was a wild dissolute youth who turned religious when he was turned down by his lady-love.' He raised his red-gold eyebrows and tipped his head forward to peer over the top of non-existent glasses before continuing. 'He wrote well over two hundred books on theology, philosophy and poetry and that's no mean feat for anyone, and even greater when one has no typewriter let alone a computer and printer to help.'

Tess smiled and nodded to show she was impressed. 'It's all right, the lecture is over for now. But,' he insisted grandly, 'you must realise that I am almost a Mallorquin. Come on,' he said, 'I'll prove it to you.' And he took her through fascinating side streets and alleys and in no time they were among the large stores in the Avenida Rey Jaime III.

'That was delicious,' Tess said and leaned back in her chair, replete. 'I have to admit, you really do know your way about Palma.' She looked around the tiny courtyard café, now full with Mallorquins leisurely lunching in this little haven of peace in the middle of the city. Some were obviously office workers, others out for a day's shopping, but all were very smartly dressed and Tess was glad she'd decided to wear her white linen skirt with a green and white blouse and matching green strappy sandals. She didn't feel too touristy in this beautiful, sophisticated city.

'This is delightful, and you wouldn't believe you're in the middle of a busy city.' Tess looked round at the abundance of plants, some hanging from balconies above, others filling large ceramic pots and said, 'This quiet, soothing atmosphere here must make the Spanish ready for their siesta. Come to think of it, I wouldn't mind one. You have fed me too well and if I were a cat I'd have a nap.'

'If you go to sleep here, love, and fall off the chair, it might be misconstrued.' She sat up straightening her back, alert once more. His crinkling eyes told her he found her amusing and she picked up her bag and excused herself.

'Ready to go now?' he asked when she returned from freshening herself in the ladies room.

'Yes. Thank you for lunch, kind sir. Dinner tonight will be my treat,' she told him.

'If you don't feel like going down to the Cathedral, I know the very place where you can rest in the shade on a lounger?' he tempted. But Tess was not sure it would be a good idea to rest and, very likely, fall asleep with Jack watching her, so she opted for the Cathedral.

They walked round then sat and soaked up the atmosphere of the impressive building and admired its fine statues and paintings, before returning for a third look at the glorious Rose Window. 'I never forgot it, you know, though it is some years since I last saw it,' Tess remarked the first time round.

'I don't suppose you ever came to the island in February or November?' She shook her head. 'You must come at least once. Where this is beautiful,' he stretched his hand towards the rainbow of colours the sun spread over the floor and furniture, 'during those months the sun is in the right position to reflect a perfect replica on the wall opposite. It's quite something.'

They were ready to leave after Tess's last look at the window and she promised, 'I will be back one November or February to see both windows.'

He smiled down into her determined face as they emerged into the bright sunshine. 'I'll underwrite the guarantee, if you like.' When he put his arm about her and squeezed her shoulder she felt cherished.

'I've had a lovely day, Jack.'

'So have I. In fact, I can't remember when I've been shopping or sightseeing and enjoyed myself as much.' He was smiling as he watched her across the teacups and Tess could see he was still in holiday mood. 'But why are we talking as though it was all over, the day isn't finished yet. You promised me dinner, remember?'

The young waitress brought the teapot and milk jug and put them beside Tess. 'Gracias.'

'Oh ho, speaking the language now?' he teased, accepting the cup she handed to him.

'I needed this,' she indicated her cup. 'That is some drive up here. You don't get the same impression on the train. Of course, Aunt Teresa and I took photos of the valley when the train made its special stop before descending to Soller.'

'When you have finished your next cup–' He pushed his own across for a refill, 'Yes, please – I will show you where we have just been.'

True to his word, as soon as she finished her second cup he paid the waitress, talking to her in her own language and, from the dimpled blush he brought to her cheeks, language was no barrier to his charm.

Outside he propelled Tess to the viewing platform for her to gasp in amazement. She could see Palma away in the distance at the farthest edge of the plain. 'It's wonderful, Jack,' she said looking up at him, then felt bashful suddenly, like a child who has found she is being watched reacting to some treat. In an attempt to hide her confusion she carried on talking. 'Look at the villages and all those grey olive trees, years and years old–'

Then she was manoeuvred until they were hidden by a gorse bush, 'Years and years old is exactly how you make me feel sometimes. But right now, I'm not old enough to control this urge.' His mouth found hers waiting and wanting. It seemed they had both learned from the kissing of a lifetime. Was it only this morning?

'Beautiful Tess, I adore you. You make me feel ten feet tall.' He gave a happy sigh as he kissed her once more, lightly, and moved back. 'I think we should go. The Spaniards are very definitely against public displays and we don't want to end in jail.' His face was full of apology as he said, 'If I could be sure Edward and party were not at Saya, I would suggest we go straight back there.' He shrugged his wide shoulders Latin fashion and led her back to look at the view again. 'I didn't give you chance to see all the hairpin bends before, but in one glance.' They both looked down.

'Quite horrifying, isn't it?' He kept the flow of chat going as he guided her to the car, 'I never think going down this side is as bad.'

He'd done it again. Thoroughly roused her, so she didn't know whether she was on foot or on horseback, then carried on as though nothing untoward had happened. It was times like these when she knew she was right out of her depth and she allowed herself to be put in the car again without a word.

As they made their way down into Soller, Tess tried to be enthusiastic about the views, but it was no good, she was completely immersed in figuring out what Jack did expect of her. Had he been sure they would be alone at Saya he'd said, then they would have gone straight there. She knew she had been accused many times of being naïve, but what exactly was she supposed to make of that?

She had already come to terms, well almost, with the fact that he was enjoying a light romantic affair with her, nothing more. She had no intention of going to bed with him, or anyone, without serious commitment on both sides. She knew she was wavering, but that was how she had always envisaged it. Her virginity was not the prize on offer in exchange for marriage, but she knew that she could not give herself totally without being sure her love was reciprocated in full.

A little shudder ran down her spine as she remembered Jack must have seen her scars, but chosen to say nothing about them. Perhaps the reminder that Edward might be at Saya, was his way of getting out of the situation they found themselves in.

'Beginning to feel tired?' he asked solicitously. 'Would you rather go straight back to Saya? I'll rustle up some food for us when we get back.' She looked up sharply then saw his slight sideways glance had caught her reaction. 'I expect you are wondering why Rosina won't get us food – I've given her and Juan a few days off. Rosina's sister is home for a holiday from America and I knew she would like a few days so all the family can be together.'

That confirmed her thoughts, but she asked anyway, 'What about Edward?'

'Edward can get his own food, I'm not feeding him.' He countered so quickly and grinned as though he'd made a joke, she didn't know what she did think anymore.

'I'm not too tired to go out to dinner in Soller,' she told him, but she felt flat – in fact, horribly depressed and far too miserable to notice Jack's concerned look.

With her eyes closed she didn't care where he took her, and didn't even open them when the car stopped and there was silence. She felt a soft breath of scented air and knew he'd opened the window on his side.

Desperate to sort herself out once and for all, Tess was very tempted to bring up the subject of her scars right this minute. Coward, she called herself, not for the first time lately, when her nerve failed.

'Jack...'

'Yes?' he prompted, when she tried to force herself. 'Are you feeling unhappy, love?' He knew – perhaps it wouldn't be so bad.

'I ... yes, I am.' Her bald statement didn't clarify anything.

'My fault?'

'No ... yes ...no. Not really, I suppose.'

'What to tell me?' He put his hand along the back of her seat and his fingers played with escaped tendrils of hair hanging down her back. Yes, oh, yes, she did want to tell him.

'It … it's nothing,' she excused. Disgust with herself almost had her groaning.

'Sure?' he soothed, not pushing for her confidence. Then he leaned closer pulling her to his chest and her head against his shoulder. 'A little cuddle might help, hmm, sweetheart?' It felt so good and she did relax. His breath in her hair and a kiss now and then, even if it was only on top of her head, worked wonders.

The orange and lemon groves around them contributed to the sweetly scented air, but Tess knew it would be the male scent of her comforter that would stay with her for always. She wanted to drink it in deeply, to fill her lungs with Jack, but she kept her breathing steady, she had some real thinking to do first.

Perhaps it was the heady perfume of this golden valley that helped her come to her decision, she didn't know, but she did know that she wanted to give the golden man holding her in his arms anything he desired of her. She also knew that she had desires, too, quite desperate desires. Somehow she had to make Jack forget her scars, forget everything that stopped him wanting to make love to her.

A few hours later, alone in her bedroom, her thoughts returned to the momentous decision. She need not have bothered. Her body was not wanted.

Jack had been his usual kind, courteous self and she had been a happy contented guest, protesting quietly when he had declared that the day was his treat and, un-less she agreed, he would take her straight home – foodless.

There was only a slight feeling of dis-appointment when she woke next morning alone. It was another lovely day and no silly thoughts were going to spoil things.

She'd have a swim before breakfast. The thought of breakfast reminded her that Rosina was visiting her family. Hard on the heels of that thought came another and she shot out of bed to pull the curtains aside.

A disappointed breath left her as she

looked out into the bay and saw a luxury motor yacht anchored there. It was quite large, not as big as the one yesterday with father and daughters, but it made a lovely picture gleaming whitely in the sunshine. It also meant that Edward and friends had arrived.

CHAPTER EIGHT

A sharp knock and the door opened before she could speak. Then, 'Sorry, Tess,' as Jack ducked back and left her standing staring. 'May I come in?' he requested.

'Yes,' she called as she hopped back into bed.

'I need a favour.' They were the last words she expected as no doubt he could see from her face. 'Have you looked out of the window this morning?'

'I've seen the boat, if that's what you mean,' she told him.

A hoot of laughter came her way and he pleaded, 'For goodness' sake don't let Rodney know you called his precious yacht a boat. But that's why I'm here in such a hurry. Will you come on to the balcony... Now, as you are?' His sense of urgency had her out of bed without a second thought and they went outside.

'Please – put your arms around me,' his voice commanded softly, but now she remembered that her T-shirt barely covered her thighs and under it she was naked – she didn't move. 'Please Tess. I'll explain.' He saw the acquiescence in her face and turned her back to the view, gathering her to him, not too close, she was relieved to note. Her arms went round his neck of their own accord, she'd made no conscious command to her limbs. With his head bent towards her, she was ready to be kissed but he was three inches away. Her eyes were not quite focussing as she looked up into tawny ones. He gave a distracted moan and pulled her to him taking her lips with his own. 'I can't resist you, Tess. Hell,' the word came out a suffering groan, and he moved their faces and bodies apart. 'Will you marry me?'

Her heart exploded into a trillion wonderful, sparkling fragments. But, 'I want to introduce you to Edward as my fiancée.' She hoped her face hadn't lit up before her gaze dropped to hide the effect his last words had on her. 'It's a bit sudden, I know, but will you?' Unusual for Jack, his voice sounded unsure. 'Edward and his party are on their way here from the yacht. I'll go down and put the coffee on.' His mouth took hers by surprise and the kiss was deepening even as he pushed himself away. 'Told you I can't resist you.' His wry grin and the light tap on her nose with a gentle finger made her feel delicious. She was still looking at the door long after he'd closed it behind himself.

Slowly walking into the bathroom, she tried to sort out exactly what had been said just now. The overall effect she was left with was disappointment. It was a game, pretend, nothing real about his proposal. Her ire began to surge upward. How dare he play about with her feelings like this?

The sound of laughter and voices greeted her when she finally went on to the terrace. For some perverse reason she was glad she had piled her hair up in a soft top knot as she took in the long, shaggy styles worn by the three beautiful girls who seemed to be all over her new fiancé. 'Tess, darling, come and meet Edward and his friends.' She was thankful to see him extract himself and come forward, smiling.

'Edward says he already knows you,' he said, watching her face, and Tess shook her head even as she glimpsed a look of recognition on his brother's face and wondered why.

'How are you, Tess? Long time no see.' The tanned young man Jack had intimated was his brother, came forward and before she could refute knowing him or do anything to prevent it, he had kissed her on the mouth. 'Mmm, sweet as always.'

'I don't–'

'Hands off, Edward. My fiancée is out of bounds.' She had struggled away from Edward even as Jack spoke loudly and clearly, drowning her words and reaction. She could almost feel the animosity crackling in the air around them, but a horrified sob broke the

149

tension and she looked round to see the dark haired girl of the trio sitting with a younger blonde either side of her, looking anxious. Then she stood, a wide smile on her lips, and came over.

'Congratulations, Jack.' Her pale face was the only clue to the fact that the unhappy noise earlier was from her. Tess couldn't help being curious about the strikingly lovely brunette. She turned to Tess, 'I'm sure you will be very happy. I'm Lorna, by the way. These fellows are not making a very good job of the introductions, are they? Babs,' she held her hand out to one of the girls as they joined her, 'and Faye – Tess? Tess,' she confirmed when Tess nodded. 'And our captain, Rodney. Come and meet Tess, Rodney,' she called to the tall, gangling young man who was hanging back, looking rather like a puppy who'd stolen a bone and was expecting trouble, Tess thought.

'Thank you, Lorna,' Jack said giving her the smile of an old friend. 'It's always good to see you. Sit down all of you and I'll pour the coffee. Babs and Faye will pass it round for me, won't you, girls.' He gave them his usual charming smile and they happily followed him to the table.

Edward came to sit beside Tess, 'How did you and Jack meet?' he asked conversationally, but she felt a tightening in the back of her neck that warned her to be very wary of this man.

'Coffee, love,' Jack came and handed her a cup. 'I have to thank you, Edward, for sending me this sweet girl. I had no idea that you were a reader of minds, able to see my ideal woman, then finding and sending her to me.' He ran his finger possessively down her nose, tapping the end as he smiled into her eyes. For the moment she was transported back to their first meeting and the spell his eyes had cast over her, unaware of her own soft look. They both missed the look his step-brother gave them.

'You sly old thing. You told me you had work to do and couldn't be disturbed.'

'That didn't stop you coming, I notice.'

The bitter note was back in Jack's voice, then it softened, 'Tess has been wonderfully relaxing and I have never worked so well. But, I'm afraid this morning is all the time we can spare you good folks.' His sorrowful, but definite tones left no doubt that he expected his guests to be gone before too long. 'If I know Rodney, he will be anxious to put to sea again fairly soon.' His strong hint was well taken when Rodney stood up and said,

'Rather.'

'Sit down, Rod, we haven't had our swim in the pool yet,' his disgruntled friend told him. 'And you know we promised the girls a dip in the famous author's pool.' It was the sneer in his voice that Tess found distasteful. He had invited himself, and friends, and was happily taking his step-brother's hospitality, yet... He's a horrible person, she decided, and it explained a lot. Strange, she didn't think Lorna looked as though she would be comfortable in such company. She looked a nice woman, very attractive in a natural way, not a bit like the two dolly bird type blondes with their miniscule bikinis and bright red shiny lips and long, long nails.

'Eddy, I want to swim now,' Babs, or was it Faye? called to him, breaking into Tess's thoughts. The girl pulled a face and pouted when she was told to wait a minute.

Tess stood up, feeling a little over dressed in her one piece suit, and said, 'What a good idea. Let's go and leave the men to bake.' A glance over her shoulder showed her the now giggling blondes shedding their tops and throwing them to their holiday companions. She was glad of her matelot suit, but noticed Lorna made no move to join them.

'Do you swim much, Tess?' one of the girls asked as she went by, swimming breast stroke with a dedication more fitting to an Olympic hopeful that a pleasurable holiday exercise. Her friend swept the water behind her with equal verve.

'Quite a bit.'

'Thought so. Those boobs look as good in that suit as though you had preformed cups.'

Heavens, what a conversation with some-one you've barely exchanged a couple of words with. She nearly laughed out loud as she imagined Kathy's reaction when she told her about this visitation.

'Marvellous exercise for the boobs, isn't it? Uh ho, here they come, Faye.' In front of Tess's eyes these hard training ladies became once again the frothy girls ready to play. She'd never seen anything like it before. It was fascinating. But it made her realise that she didn't know as much about people and life as she thought.

Tess continued her swim happily ignoring the other four, who were now indulging in horse play, but a niggle in her mind kept wondering where Lorna and Jack were. Had he gone back to work? She knew that was silly to even think it – his good manners would never allow it. And if Lorna chose to stay up on the terrace, he would feel obliged to stay with her. He might prefer to stay with her, to be alone with her...

Her strokes became stronger now as she

increased her speed, using freestyle she powered up and down the pool. What did she do now? Surely he wasn't already regretting that he had asked her to pretend to be his fiancée? Very likely. And very likely he was explaining it all to Lorna right this very minute. And when she got out of this pool she was going to feel a right charley. She could feel the heat in her cheeks already.

She didn't hear the scream.

Someone had dropped a ton weight on her head, but someone else was pulling her from under it – into the sunlight once again. Pulling her up and up. Jack. She'd know the feel of those arms anywhere as they carried her, then laid her down on a soft bed. His warm lips were kissing her face in between crooning soft words that she couldn't quite take in, then nothing...

The hospital insisted she stay in overnight as a precaution, since she had lost consciousness for a time, but Rodney was allowed out with a cover over his stitched eyebrow and instructions to take it easy for two or three days.

Opening her eyes, she could see from the slant of the shadows in her room that it was late in the day. She must have been asleep for some time. Turning her head slightly, she saw Jack. He was slumped, eyes closed, in an armchair, his hair quite fiery as it caught the rays of the sun, but he looked so worn out that she forgot anything else. Poor Jack, had he been sitting here for hours? Should she wake him up and tell him to go home? Or should she let him sleep a little longer? There was a muted crash from the corridor and he woke up, looking across to Tess, anxiety plain to see, as though he thought the noise was her falling out of bed.

She tried not to let the wince show as she smiled at him. 'Hello.'

'Hello, yourself. How do you feel, love?' His smile looked a bit forced as he came over to the bed. 'Fit enough to kiss your fiancé?'

'There's no need...' He didn't let her finish as his mouth came down on hers and

156

worked its usual magic, but oh, so gently.

'There's every need, Tess, Teresa, Summers.'

'Jack, you do believe I didn't know Edward before, don't you?' The earnest husky voice surprised herself and she realised she must have been worrying about Edward trying to pretend he already knew her.

'Don't worry, Tess, I know my step-brother and I know you. I–' The door opened quickly but silently as a nurse came in.

'Thank you for ringing,' she said to Jack. 'How are you feeling, Tess?' The enquiry accompanied her taking Tess's wrist between her fingers and lifting the watch pinned to her breast.

'I'll see you later, dear,' and Jack left.

'I really am all right, Jack.' Tess laughed at her unintentional joke as she tried to reassure him. He was driving her home after her overnight stop, 'I felt a terrible fraud this morning, the headache had gone and I'm as fit as a flea.'

157

'The Doctor said you're to take it easy.' His no nonsense tone brooked no argument and he carried on, 'And I think it might be as well if you keep to your room for a day or so, at least until we're rid of Edward's lot. Not that I've seen much of them since the idiot shoved Rodney on top of you.'

'Come on, Jack, it was an accident...'

'Yes, but if Edward doesn't know by now that you don't fool about near pools, well...' They drove in silence for the rest of the way home and Tess wondered how Lorna had fared with the others obviously paired off. But Jack would have been there last night for company for her. The thought was not a happy one and she switched to look at the scenery before closing her eyes.

'Te.e.ss. We're home, sweetheart.' The gentle voice brought her back to reality and she opened her eyes to find Jack lifting her out of the low slung car.

'I can manage,' though her croaky voice showed more than words that she had been sound asleep. But she was wide awake now,

'Truly, Jack, I can manage.' He put her down but kept his arm about her and the other holding her elbow to make sure she got up the steps without mishap. The memory of the first time she had entered the hall came clearly to her as she looked at the sweeping staircase, but this time Lorna was at the top smiling a welcome. She came down as Jack picked Tess up.

'It's no good protesting, I'm carrying you to bed.' But before he could move Rosina came bustling into the hall and seeing Tess her face creased in concern and she spoke rapidly, albeit unintelligibly, to the invalid.

'She says she is happy to see you home and sorry about the accident,' Lorna translated for Tess.

'Rosina, you shouldn't have come back so soon. What about your sister?'

Again Lorna translated her reply before Jack could say a word. However, he spoke rapidly to the housekeeper, nodded his thanks to Lorna and carried Tess to her room.

'I feel as though I've been away months,' she told him as he put her on her feet.

'You have,' was his cryptic reply. He went over to her sitting room door and opened it wide. 'I still think you would be wise to stay up here. I have locked the other door, this sitting room is yours.' She understood better when he said, 'Edward's girl – can't tell one from the other – is in The Room.' The scowl left his face when he raised those eyebrows and looked at her knowingly.

'Oh, dear.' She shuddered at the thought of the claustrophobic white puffball of a room she had seen when she first arrived at Saya, then went into the pleasant little sitting room. 'I think you could be right, Jack. This peaceful atmosphere suits the way I feel at the moment.' She sat down on the sofa. Before she could blink he had pulled a stool forward then lifted her feet up on it.

He seemed to be standing not doing any-thing in particular and not knowing what to do – so unlike himself she had to say some-thing. 'Jack, for heaven's sake, what is the matter with you?' He didn't say, only gave her a gentle smile. 'You don't need to stay with me when you've work to do. Or see to your other guests or whatever it is that is bothering you.' Her forthright words had little or no effect on him. She began to feel alarmed and couldn't keep the bite from her voice. 'Jack, do you want me to guess what's wrong, or are you going to tell me?'

He sat down, balancing on the stool beside her feet, and leaning forward he took hold of her hands. Tess wished now she had ignored the lines grooving his face. She didn't think she wanted to hear what he was going to say. 'If you'd rather not say...'

'I still haven't had our word framed, have I? But I need to use it again – Tess, I'm sorry I got you into this situation. I had no right to ask you...'

'Don't say it. I understand, really I do. You want out of this mock engagement–'

'Hell, no,' he declared emphatically. Tess felt lighter – perhaps things weren't so bad. There was a faint shriek from outside –

Babs, or Faye – and Jack nodded his head towards it. 'I should have locked the doors on the playgroup and stayed in bed all day yesterday.' The thought of Jack hiding from anyone amused her and he gave her a healthy leer. 'Preferably yours.' An inward sigh washed through her, that was more like her Jack. She returned him an encouraging little smile.

'Tell me, is my head all that's bothering you? You looked horribly worried just now that I thought something major was wrong.'

'I am concerned for you, naturally,' he said squeezing her hands, 'but there are one or two things that don't add up.' He shrugged his shoulders. 'Now is not the time to think about them. You must rest, my dear, you're beginning to look tired.'

'Thank you, kind sir, that's exactly what a woman needs to know.' But he was right, she did feel weary and she should have felt relieved when he left her, recommending she get in to bed properly.

When she woke a couple of hours later she lay in bed trying to figure out which were the things that didn't add up. The most glaring one she could see was Edward's greeting. There was no way he had met her before and she not remember, yet he'd implied they were friendly – almost more than that. He was definitely one to be on guard against. On the very slight acquaintance she had with him, she could see he was a manipulator, using people as though they were pieces in his chess game. Altogether a thoroughly nasty person. That was sure to be one of the things to be talked about when Jack came back.

It had been fun when they'd had Saya to themselves, talking and discussing all manner of things. Sometimes they got quite heated – well, she did – but it had never spoiled their evening. That pleasant time seemed long gone now, though it could only be two or three days ago. She shook off the feeling of loss and tried to think what else Jack had on his mind. Lorna?

On cue there was a knock on her door and Lorna looked in. 'Good, you are awake. Jack thought you might still be sleeping, but I said if you were awake you were probably dying for a cup of tea.' She smiled good-naturedly and brought the cup over to Tess, who struggled up to take it, very conscious of her T-shirt. She just knew that Lorna would wear sleek silk satin nighties and never look tired! Yes, she admitted, she was jealous. Just how well did Jack know Lorna? 'Thank you, that was kind. I'll drink it then have another nap for a half hour or so.'

She knew she was being less than gracious but if this attractive woman stayed any longer, she was likely to ask what she was to Jack.

CHAPTER NINE

'Good idea, my dear.' Lorna left still smiling her kind smile.

Don't patronise me, Tess screamed silently to the door. All she wanted to do was throw herself back on the pillows and pull the sheet over her head and bawl her eyes out.

Throwing back the sheet she took a few deep breaths – then felt light headed. Just why was Lorna here? It was plain to see that she and Jack were old friends. Tess wished she had been there when the cruise party arrived and Jack saw Lorna with them. Without looking for signs she'd seen that Lorna was the odd one out there. Much more mature and sure of herself than any of the others – the men were certainly not in her league. But Jack is!

Pain inflicted by a sharp knife was how she

would have described the pain in her chest. Lorna was here for Jack. The hurt cry when he introduced her, Tess, as his fiancée had come from the sort of pain she had just experienced. Poor Lorna. Poor me. What a mess.

Where was Jack? She needed to know what he was thinking and feeling in this morass. Was all this some scheme dreamed up in the nasty little mind of Edward? Never had she come anywhere near such people as these.

Her biggest problem, she was ready to admit, was her terrible imagination. It kept ignoring the knowledge that there was no chance of permanency with Jack – in spite of seeing the evidence every time she undressed. Tess jumped on her unhappy thoughts and began packing her few belongings.

A knock startled her – Jack? Faye's head poked round the door this time. It was worse than Piccadilly Circus here, but she put a smile of welcome on her face. 'I didn't know if you were still sleeping,' the girl said apologetically, slipping into the room.

'Nope, I'm OK now, thanks,' and waited to hear what Faye had come for.

'I hope you don't mind me coming to see you like this,' she said rather nervously. 'Only Rodney is in such a state to know exactly how you are – and quite honestly, Jack is frightening him to death by what he's not saying,' she ended in a rush.

'Oh, dear, poor Rodney. Well, you can tell him to stop worrying – I'm fine.'

'Do you … would you mind if he came to see for himself?'

'He must be in a state if he won't believe you,' Tess smiled sympathetically, 'But, by all means tell him to come to my sitting room, next door.' She indicated the wall with her head and Faye went off at a dash, thanking her as she went.

Well, well, well, curiouser and curiouser. And she went next door to soak up the quiet ambience of the little room while she waited for her partner in accident, if there was such

167

a phrase.

Walking to the window, she looked down at the pool for the first time since she'd been pulled out of it the day before. Edward and Babs were not in sight, but Rodney and Faye were talking as they lay in the sunshine, very relaxed. So much for the life and death – cloak and dagger stuff.

She looked to the other end of the pool terrace and there were Jack and Lorna, sitting close together chatting away, not a care in sight. So much for thinking he was worried about her. He couldn't care less, unless Lorna reassured him so well he thinks he doesn't need to. She dragged her eyes away from the twosome only to look back instantly to confirm that Jack had hold of Lorna's hand with both of his! With a bit of hard fighting she beat her baser self into submission and declared aloud that as soon as she'd seen Rodney, she would go and phone for a taxi. Meanwhile, and thereafter, she would keep to her room until her transport arrived.

Faye and Rodney were getting up and casually walking to the steps – Tess turned away from the window. In the bedroom she checked her passport and ticket were to hand and just hoped she would be able to change her flight without too much trouble. It was essential to get away today.

Voices sounded in the corridor and she hurried through to open the door to them. This was a different couple to the pair she'd seen coming towards the house, and said so.

'I told Rod he had to behave casually or Jack would suspect. That's why we couldn't come straight back up.'

'What on earth do you think he'd do?' Tess asked them incredulously.

'My God,' Rodney said and shuddered, 'You've never seen Jack Luff in a rage or you wouldn't ask.' Heavens, Tess felt herself blanche and sat down, waving to the others to sit. She had just spent nearly three weeks virtually alone with a... But she almost laughed out loud when she saw Faye helping Rodney down on to the sofa before sitting beside him and patting his hand.

Shaking her head, she said, 'I don't think I can have, Rodney. But tell me, what is he likely to do?'

Poor Rodney, he clearly was suffering, just remembering previous bouts of Jack's rage, but he manfully spoke up, 'He roars like a raging bull, Tess. It's truly terrible. And the words he uses – I don't always understand them – but the noise is fearsome, I do assure you.' He shuddered again in Faye's arms that she had wrapped round to protect him. 'So you see, my dear, though I did want to see you to tell you how sorry I am for the accident, I … I … well you do see?'

Yes, she did see, but Faye had him well in hand and Tess sent him away feeling much better now he'd seen for himself that she would live.

Right, phrase book, 'I need a taxi, immediately'.

Going down the stairs, her eyes and ears finely tuned for signs of Jack, Tess caught sight of his white sports car speeding off down the drive. Unable to stop the gasp of dismay when she recognised Lorna sitting in *her* seat, she leaned against the window frame, following the car with her eyes.

That was a bit of luck. She could walk down the rest of the stairs with no fear of bumping into anyone who mattered. And use the telephone – no problem. At least when she found Rosina and asked her how the phone system worked here on Majorca – no problem! And it made no difference to her that Jack had taken his old friend out for a drive as soon as *she* came home from hospital...

Rosina was a real help and seemed to understand that Tess wanted to go to the airport as soon as possible. The housekeeper arranged for a taxi to come immediately, or so Tess deduced from the odd word she understood in the one sided conversation. Tess's gratitude was waved away as Rosina cheerfully got back to preparing the evening meal.

There didn't seem any point in finding the others to say goodbye, but she wrote a little note and left it on her bedside table, addressing it to Senor Luff. In it she expressed her appreciation of all he had done for her and his forebearance in allowing her to stay when he was finishing his final draft. She wished him luck with the publication. Not adding that she ached to know if he wrote under his own name so she could look out for it and buy it to remind her of the most precious time of her life.

With her carry all over her shoulder and hefting her canvas roll bag she struggled down the stairs to be ready for when the taxi came. She was feeling a bit anxious now, not knowing where Jack and Lorna had gone, and for all she knew they might be back any minute.

The taxi arrived and, wide eyed, Tess took in every second of the journey to the airport. She thought she knew how a condemned man must feel, yet she could still smile a little at her stupid imagination – there was no reason for her never to return to Majorca. She just knew she never would.

The airport, as always, was very busy and she laboured through the crowds with her luggage trolley to get to the information counter. She needed to see how to change her ticket so she could go home today.

There was a queue and she had no alternative but to join it. Thankfully she didn't have to carry her bags and looked about her as she waited. Her scalp tightened in alarm, then she forced herself to relax. She would have to get used to that – seeing Jack, or rather, men who reminded her of him. She didn't like to look towards the ferocious frown she'd glimpsed between heads across the huge hall, but it had been so like her first sight of Jack, her face softened in a little smile.

'Thank you, Miss Summers. I suppose you left a note telling me goodbye?' She froze. The cold voice was his; the frown was not only like the original, it was the original. She turned, determined not to panic – not to be talked down to.

'Why, Jack, I'm glad you found me,' she lied. 'I saw you and Lorna going out, so, yes, I did leave a note for you.' She looked beyond him, 'Is Lorna with you?' That was all she needed to make her departure complete, but she tried to smile cheerfully. 'I suddenly felt I wanted to go home,' she said, hoping he would understand a bout of homesickness and not demand too much in the way of explanation.

'Lorna has gone.' Was that unhappiness? 'I won't keep you long–' There was no need to tell her, she already knew that. '–come and have a coffee.'

'But I'll lose my place,' she protested as he went off with the trolley, then picked up her bags as he parked it and came back to her when she hadn't moved. He didn't look too pleased and she was reminded of poor Rodney – not that she would let him intimidate her like that. Love him she might, but out of his own mouth had come the words, 'Having all one's own way is not character building.'

He looked considering at her, 'What exactly are you trying to find out?' When she told him he said, 'That's no problem, I can give you all the information you need. Come on.' She went – people were beginning to take an interest in them. Anyway, perhaps it was weak to want to be with this grumpy, lovely man for a while longer, but she couldn't help herself.

'Hey, where are you taking me?' she demanded trying to stop walking, but he had hold of her arm and a fair speed going as they went outside.

'I'm sure you wouldn't want other people to hear what I have to say to you, Tess, so we're going to sit in the car.'

Dread and excitement had her imagination whizzing round too fast to capture, but an alarm sounded in her head when he opened the boot of his car and put her bags in. Her mouth was open to demand he took them out right now, when he pointed out, 'They'll be safer in there, than leaving them outside,' his hand already opening the passenger door for her.

Trying to show she was not about to be browbeaten, she got in and turned to face him when he was sitting beside her. 'You had something to say,' she stated, and waited.

'I suppose Edward's paid you off.'

Whatever she might have imagined, it wasn't that and it took several seconds of stunned silence for her to come up with an answer.

'And I suppose it is because you are a writer that you must look for twists in the plot,' she spoke precisely, not showing him he had shattered her.

Her mind sizzled with a new idea – should she use it? It was the perfect get out. All she had to do was say 'yes' and 'goodbye'. But her innate honesty wouldn't allow her to lie to him. She couldn't bear for him to think all their time together had been a sham.

He seized the implication, but he'd already felt the shaft of pain from her eyes, 'Why are you leaving then?'

'I thought you didn't want me.'

'Tess.'

Just her name, but his voice held the staff of life for her. The desperate longing echoed in her very soul. How could she leave him? He loved her. Did he love her enough? She stopped the doubt and went into his open arms to be wrapped close and held as though time had no dimension. The comfort was wonderful, but after a time she needed to be kissed and bestirred herself to find his mouth. Comfort turned to sheer joy as their lips met and tongues mingled. He held her face in both hands to kiss her eyes, nose, chin, then nibbled tender lips. She opened her mouth to capture his. Breathless, they came up for air, smiling with love.

'Darling, you are coming home with me, aren't you.' It should have been a question but it came out a statement. And she didn't care if she should demand he ask, not tell her – she didn't want him humble. Her sea-green eyes were shining as she looked into beloved hazel ones and nodded her head.

They drove up to the house behind a taxi

and Tess saw Edward get out, then Babs, carrying bags proclaiming ladies wear from several exclusive boutiques in Palma. 'Hi, there,' the pretty blonde called and holding up the plasticized carriers said, 'We've had a wonderful day. You been shopping?'

'Just a drive out,' Jack answered for them both. His arm was round her waist now they were on the steps and he guided her up to the door. 'I'll fetch your things in a minute,' he whispered in her ear, smiling down at her as though he were whispering sweet nothings. Her glance showed him she appreciated his thoughtfulness as he moved her towards the 'Hollywood' staircase.

There was nothing soft about his voice when he spoke to his step-brother, 'Edward, a word if you please. My office in ten minutes.' and he was gone, making it obvious it was not open for negotiation.

Walking along the upper corridor with the couple, Tess heard Edward say to Babs, 'I'll be along in a tick – just got to see Rodders. As well I decided we should move on, I think.' He shrugged his shoulders under the linen jacket and turned back the way they had come, but not before he'd given Tess a calculating glance and an odd smile.

'See you later, Babs,' she said and turned to go into her sitting room. Babs followed her into the doorway.

'I wondered what was the other side of the door. Have you seen my room? It's fabulous. Faye was real jealous when she saw it. Eddy said he had it done specially for me.'

'Did he?' Then thought it might be as well to pretend she hadn't seen the room – it would save questions. 'What is fabulous about it?'

Entreated to come and look, she nearly gave the game away by making for the adjoining door, but Babs was already out and going to The White Room. She flung open the door and stood to one side for Tess to enter and admire. Fortunately she was so thrilled that Tess didn't need to say a thing except a word or two of agreement. Nevertheless she was glad to escape back to her own little haven.

A noise in her bedroom sent her rushing from the sitting room. 'Oh, it's you,' she told Jack, much relieved.

'And who might it have been, that would have you storming in?' She went into his arms quite naturally and gave her lips up for a soothing kiss.

'I suppose I'm letting my imagination loose again, but I don't trust your step-brother. I have this feeling that he will try to pay us – you – back for not being upset when he had had every intention that you should be.'

'Don't worry about Edward, I shall deal with him in,' he looked at his watch, 'about four minutes.'

With Jack gone she emptied her bags and put everything back where it had been before.

A soft glow of anticipation spread right through her system as she prepared herself for the evening and by the time she was ready with only her 'just in case' dress to slip on, she was having to dampen her yearning to rush downstairs to see Jack again.

She turned eagerly at the sound of her door opening, 'You!' and she stepped back as Edward came into the room closing the door behind him.

'Well, if it isn't our Victorian Miss.' It was clear he hadn't come to apologise to her for getting her into Jack's villa uninvited and continued, 'all ready and waiting.' Then he turned, twisting the key in the lock. Alarm slithered down her back, but she fought to keep control as he looked her up and down and moved slowly towards her.

Rapidly gathering her scattered wits, she cast a cold eye over him, 'My God, what makes you think I'd ever be ready for you, when there's a real man like Jack Luff about,' she added, even as she despised herself for saying something as foul to anybody. That it could have been the wrong tactic she knew when he stopped and a murderous look came into his eyes. Fear changed the perspiration down her spine to ice – if she moved it would surely splinter.

While she watched, his expression changed yet again to falsely charming but her body kept its rigidity. 'Now, Tess, or should I call you Teresa? – that's no way to speak to your benefactor, is it? After all, it's not every unknown author who gets the chance to spend a month alone with a rich publisher.'

Something was wrong here, surely he meant author. Jack was a writer not a publisher.

'I think you had better leave, Edward. You tried to do damage but you failed. I don't know how or why you picked on me and I don't want to. It's not important.' She would have loved to fling open the door theatrically and wait for him to exit, but he was standing between her and it. 'Other things are. Fact one – Jack and I love each other. Fact two – you are not going to spoil it.'

Surely she'd seen that expression in nature films – on a snake about to strike. Dreadful fascination kept her rigid and mute.

'Don't you want to know what Jack and I

have been talking about, Teresa? I think you should. I could save you getting in too deep. And I feel I should do something for my favourite old teacher. You are related to Miss Summers who taught at Merryhew, aren't you?' Things clicked into place. People said she looked like her aunt, but he was carrying on – his voice thick with pleasure, 'For instance, did you know Lorna and Jack have this on-going thing? He strays but she comes running every time he's finished with the *friend* of the moment. We got our timing wrong this time – pity. She had a wasted journey, but he knows she will be there when he's ready. Good old Lorna – faithful little thing, ain't she?'

CHAPTER TEN

Sickened, Tess listened as he warmed to his theme. A further tightening inside her said there was a possibility he could be speaking the truth, but commonsense overruled the stabbing jealousy. 'You've made your point. Now please leave me alone.' Her commonsense continued its task as she made her voice sound defeated, wanting him to believe his poison was effective. She chanced turning her back on him and sat at her desk, dejected, her head in her hands. Every nerve ending alive and acting as antennae, terrified he wouldn't go, but come and touch her.

The closing of the door made her head swivel so fast she cricked her neck, but it was a welcome pain when she saw her empty room. Rushing over she locked the door, then checking the door to the sitting room was locked, she stripped off her clothes and got under the shower again to rid her body of the sweat his noxious presence had caused. She was trembling so violently when she came out she couldn't think of dressing and wrapped the soft grey robe tightly round her.

How long she sat huddled in the chair she didn't care, but when she heard Babs' high pitched voice through her balcony window calling goodbye, she did get up to look. She was in time to see the hated Edward and his girl friend walking down to the beach path. Babs was carrying the same bags she had brought in earlier and he had some pieces of luggage. Thank God. The relief she felt showed her just how much that vile person had got to her and she shook her head in disbelief.

A strong knock and Jack's voice at the door, sped her to open it and fling herself at him. 'Very nice,' she heard the smile in his voice and with his arms about her, she felt safe. 'Mmm, nice to be welcomed like this,' he teased and put her away so he could see her face. His lost its amiability, 'What is it? What's the matter?' He gave her a little shake when she didn't answer. 'Tess?' She swallowed; she didn't want to tell him what Edward had said.

'Edward came in ... and locked the door–'

'What?' She shook her head to show him nothing physical had happened.

'He didn't touch me, just ... he ... he frightened me...' The warmth of Jack's arms gave her strength, 'I'm sure he's unhinged. I'm sorry, I suppose I shouldn't say that to you, after all he is your brother...'

'Don't think twice about that, love. I've known him a long time and believe me he hasn't improved with knowing.' His calm, quiet voice made her feel better. He kissed her tenderly and said, 'Do you feel like coming down for dinner?' His smile was reassuring. 'Dinner for two again – should be bliss?' She nodded. 'I'll leave you to dress – not that I wouldn't be happy to dine with you like that – the choice is yours.' His cheeky grin with those raised eyebrows lightened her heart and she kissed him then pushed him towards the door.

'I think we have been here before...' His gravelly voice whispered in her ear, as she felt the cool air on her bare back.

'Jack Luff.' Then the zip slid up to the top and he chewed her sensitised ear lobe before turning her round and kissing her more satisfactorily. Tess broke away, noticing as she did so that he had changed his shirt again. When she commented on these peacocking author's with nothing to do but try on clothes, she was chased out on to the terrace where their evening meal was set.

It was when Jack poured her wine that she noticed his knuckles were badly grazed. 'Oh, what on earth have you done? How did it happen?' she wanted to know.

He looked quite sheepish as he answered, 'It's nothing. Just caught my hand on something.'

'You'd lie to me? Some friend you are.'

'No need for the scolding – I did catch my hand on something.'

'Did you wash it well? It might have got dirt in.'

'I did wash it and even put antiseptic on it,' he told her piously. 'It so happens it was a particularly nasty thing I hit.'

'Hit?' she echoed, 'You accidentally hit something?'

'I didn't say it was accidental.' He looked on the table, 'More broccoli?'

'No, thank you. If it wasn't accidental, then what happened?' But she thought she already knew.

'I don't think you need to know more than Edward departed looking for a dentist in case his teeth are loose. And I'm pretty sure he will decide not to shave for a few days,' he told her simply but with relish, adding, 'The best bit is that Rodney had already given orders to weigh anchor, and I don't anticipate seeing any of that quartet for a good long time. Satisfied?'

'Yes, but–'

'You're not satisfied.'

'I am, truly, but–' Jack heaved a big sigh but she persisted, '–but how did you get to the boat?'

'Ah. Had the good fortune to catch Edward about to embark in the outboard. He and Babs had had to wait until Rodney saw them on the beach and sent it to pick them up. I'm surprised you didn't hear her squealing up here. He's learnt the hard way not to frighten my beautiful fiancée.' He had warmed to his theme and sounded very pleased with himself. Secretly, Tess couldn't help being very pleased with him, too.

'Thank you,' she said, stretching out her hand to touch his.

'Ouch!' The fighter of dragons instantly became poor injured little scrap. 'You can kiss me better later.' The lovely twinkle was back in his eyes and she felt beautiful.

Later, 'Better now?' her concern did her credit she thought.

'Not quite.' And he pushed her head close

so his lips could regain possession of hers. 'Tess, darling, I adore you. I just can't get enough of you.' 'Mmm,' she agreed, but there were questions she wanted answering now – they had agreed not to talk about anything nasty while they ate.

'Jack,' she said, putting space between them, 'I think we should carry on walking for a while. You haven't told me yet if Edward said how he happened to use me for this charade, when he meant it to be Aunt Teresa.' It bothered her quite a bit and it showed in her voice.

'OK, my love, I'll tell you the whole sordid business.' His distaste was clear. 'Apparently, when your Aunt Teresa took early retirement last year Edward saw a piece in the local rag about her and remembered her from his schooldays. And clearly his tiny mind schemed to get at me by sending an old retired schoolmarm–'

'–Old? Teresa isn't old.'

'It's possible small boys would think anyone over the age of twenty-five was old,' he reasoned.

'Hmm, but I distinctly remember my invitation said it was a good place for writers, and Aunt Teresa doesn't write anything, except letters, of course.' Her frown cleared, 'Now, I remember. The article said she might write a book about her experiences – Teresa was only joking with the reporter when she said that.'

"That's another little mystery out of the way. Anything else?' he asked flippantly, not expecting one.

'Er, I, er know it really was only Edward's spite, but ... Lorna...' She felt his arm about her stiffen.

'What did that horrible little runt have to say about Lorna?'

'Please don't be cross with me...'

'I'm not, love, but Edward isn't fit to lick her shoes.'

A quiver slithered through her. 'He said she was someone special and that she always forgave you and took you back when you ... strayed.' They were on the soft sand now they'd come off the path and walking wasn't so easy, but she was glad they still had their arms about each other.

'Lorna is special–'

Tess carried on walking, managing to contain her agony.

'–I've known her for years. She was married to my best friend, but he was killed not long after they married – mugger with a knife in New York when he was on business.' Tess hugged him closer before he carried on, 'There have been times when I did wonder whether we might make a go of it, but something always held me back. I know now what it was.' He stopped and took her in his arms to show her what he meant. His kisses reassured her as much as his words, but she wanted to hear the rest. 'Believe me, I never even hinted to Lorna, though I took her out now and again; parties, the theatre…'

Tess knew he wasn't aware that Lorna was in love with him. Poor Lorna. Tess hoped she would find someone else to love.

'Any more problems we should sort out?

Or do you think...?' The light hearted note gave him away and she could see his teeth gleaming in the dark as he laughed and said hopefully, 'Or can we go back inside now?'

They turned and retraced their steps in companionable silence, stopping now and again as they neared a cicada, then using a finger to point the direction they guessed it would start again. This silent game saw them on the terrace in no time and Tess looked back at the bay with a half moon illuminating its sparkling expanse. 'Look, it's empty.' She looked up at Jack beside her, his face was lit by the soft outdoor lighting. 'I didn't notice before...' her voice trailed off as his head came down.

'Tess,' the low gravelly sound set her body instantly aflame. 'Darling,' and he swept her into his arms kissing her mouth, her eyes and ears, before returning to her seeking mouth and giving it the satisfaction it craved.

She didn't want him to stop, but a tiny dark cloud entered her head and she knew there was something she must say. With difficulty she moved away.

'What is it, sweetheart?' His love softened features smiled at her and her heart turned over, but she knew she must say it, now.

'Jack … I … I … there's something you should know.' A cold hand gripped her heart as she watched his face change and become the expressionless countenance she dreaded seeing.

'Yes?' his low voice prompted and she had to steel herself to continue.

'I should have told you before … I know you're a perfectionist…'

'I like to think so.'

That lead weight was back at the bottom of her stomach. 'I think you should know before we go any further – you might not want to after you know…'

'Really?' The indifferent sound almost floored her.

'I … I was in a train accident some years ago…' She stopped and looked about her, licking her lips. 'It … it killed my mother

and father and brother and…' She put her
hand up to keep him away, 'and I wasn't
badly injured, only trapped from the waist
down and had to be cut free,' she finished in
a hurry, but didn't look at him, afraid of
what she would read in his eyes and still not
able to say about her scars…

Jack took her hand and pulled her back to
his chest, kissing the top of her head. 'My
poor darling,' he murmured softly. 'Are you
worried about your scars? Is that what's
troubling you?' he asked gently.

Her head jerked back as the bonds that
held her snapped and she nodded. 'How did
you know?'

It was his turn to look away, but only for a
second then she saw his expression, the one
she thought of as his little boy look, that
said, I've been bad but you won't be cross
will you? She raised her eyebrows and
pursed her lips as she joined in the game.

'You remember my bird watching binoculars?' She nodded. 'Well, early one morning
I was watching and happened to glance

through the trees to the beach, and I saw the most beautiful sight…' She remembered commenting in his study, that one could see the beach, but she had forgotten.

'You mean you watched me?' He couldn't fail to hear the indignation in her voice.

'Please, Tess, don't make me sound like some dirty old voyeur getting kicks from spying on young girls.' She hadn't thought that and said so, trying to sound reasonable.

'I suppose I should have resisted the temptation, but you were so beautiful as you stretched your arms out to the sun and spread your hair to dry.'

Sure his self-reproach was genuine she hugged him swiftly and smiled her forgiveness. 'And you saw my scars.'

He looked anxiously into her eyes. 'Do you mind very much?'

She shook her head, the last little cloud had gone. He didn't mind. Jack had released her from a lifetime's anxiety she had only vaguely been aware of. 'Thank you,' she whispered and couldn't stop the tears of liberation pouring down her face.

'Don't cry,' his voice cracked as he gathered her to him. 'Please, love, I'm sorry if I've upset you. I shouldn't have looked. Heaven knows it was exquisite torture, but I loved you so much and dare not touch you, except for a small kiss now and again.' She heard the desperation in his voice and sniffed while he wiped her tears with a wet hand. Leaning her head against his chest she pressed her lips to it before she began.

'I think I must always have feared no one could love me with such scars.' He made a deprecating sound as though he would stop her words, but she needed to tell him. 'I was eleven when my parents died and when I came out of hospital Aunt Teresa had me to live with her. She gave me a wonderful home, but when I started at my new school, my scars were still very visible. I dreaded stripping off with the rest of the girls and going in the communal showers after games and things.' Jack kept quiet, letting her talk it out and she carried on, unaware of the distant look in her eyes. 'Some of the girls were very kind, but others made my life miserable for a long time.'

She looked up at him and gave him a heartening smile. 'I honestly thought I had forgotten all about the scars until Richard–'

'–Richard?' Jack cut in, 'But I ... you...'

Tess heaved a big sigh. 'Are you ever going to trust me?' And she was glad he had the grace to look ashamed. 'Richard is also a perfectionist,' she stressed strongly, 'But I didn't realise just how much, until one day when he told me he thought I would look good in a brief bikini we saw in a shop window.' She stopped for a second, looking into the past. Jack lifted her chin so she could see the love in his eyes now. 'I said I very much doubted it because of my scars. And from then on he was quite strange, telling me how he'd always thought of me as the perfect woman, untainted by man or imperfections. He was always a bit odd, I suppose, but having known him as my aunt's boss as I grew up, I just accepted it. Anyway,' she rushed on, 'after learning of my defects he didn't want me near him, almost as though he might catch something. Even work – told me he wouldn't expect me back in the office and I should try to write the book he knew I was struggling with. He had the cheek to tell me that that way I might do one job well instead of two jobs not so well!' A flash of acrimony sparked at the memory. 'I told you, that was why I accepted the offer of the villa, thinking it was his way of making reparation for unfair dismissal.' Now there was real anger on Jack's face.

'Good God, what sort of a man is he?'

'Not much of one, I'm afraid. But enough of him and things that don't matter. Tell me, in spite of having me here, you have worked well, haven't you?'

His wry grin was back. 'Oh, yes, my darling. I told myself that I had to finish my work before I could try to make you mine – make you love me as I love you.' He bent his head and kissed her lovingly.

'Ah, the discipline of the dedicated writer,'

she teased pertly. Then remembered Edward's slip. 'Do you know, your step-brother actually got it wrong.' She exulted in the ferocious frown she knew was for his nasty relation. 'He was so busy telling me how grateful I should be to him; he tried to tell me you were a rich publisher. Heaven knows what he thought that would achieve!' She snorted and carried on, 'He said that as an unpublished writer, I was deeply indebted to him for arranging that I spend a month alone with a "rich publisher".' She laughed up into his face, but the expression could only be guilt – 'Jack?' She watched him. 'You're not a writer!' A *frisson* of doubt ran through her.

'Yes, I am, love. And I am a publisher.' Standing in front of her he said seriously, 'Tess, I can imagine what you're thinking. There have been too many odd incidents since you arrived here, and this is just the latest in a string of lies and half-truths.' He looked into her face earnestly, 'Please believe me, I didn't deliberately not tell you about my publishing firm. Nor talk about my writing for any other reason than I never divulge my pseudonym when I first meet anyone. Then it was a game to tease you and hear you defend my writing.'

Light dawned. 'John Chaucer?' He nodded. 'That explains all those books.' He was smiling now and she remembered how hotly she had argued with him when he slighted her favourite author.

'Am I forgiven?'

'How come you're a publisher as well?' She wanted to know everything before she released him from his tenterhooks.

'My grandfather,' he moved his arm indicating the bay, 'the one who lived here, was the publisher. He wanted me to go into the firm, but I wanted to write. He was not happy about it and said he would never publish my work. I was young and very sure of myself and said I wouldn't let him.' His reminiscent smile showed how much he had loved his grandfather and no real rift had blighted their close relationship. It gave her a warm feeling to see it.

'However, after my second successful novel came out, my grandfather persuaded my agent that I was not getting a good enough deal with the publisher I was with, so we changed over. I still didn't go into the firm, it was only when Grandfather became ill, that I promised I would. We have a very good team and I don't need to be there all that much. Elaine and I inherited the company after he died.' Tess squeezed his hand, she knew from her own experience that one didn't forget loved ones.

Jack smiled at her, 'Now, any more doubts we need to clear up?'

'I don't think so, how about you?'

'Just one. When are you going to marry me?'

'I think you missed a bit out. Like – will you marry me? Should definitely come before the when.' She wrinkled her brow thoughtfully as though discussing a manuscript. But she was startled when he got down on one knee and held a hand to his heart and the other he held out to her in appeal. 'Miss Teresa Summers, will you do me the honour of becoming me bride?' He twirled his non-existent moustache.

'Idiot, the moustache belongs to the villain,' she laughed. 'Of course I will.'

'Is that a yes?' But he knew the answer and lifted her off her feet kissing her as only he knew how. Tess was almost delirious with happiness when they parted, smiling their love for each other.

'I meant it for real when I asked you last time, but our "guests" were already ashore and I thought I needed more time to convince you to spend the rest of your life with me.' That look in his eyes and she was ready to melt. 'Oh, Tess, you are perfect.'

'As perfect as the mermaid you're looking for?'

'Don't you know? I found my mermaid some time ago. I fell in love and drowned in her sea-green eyes.' Her insides fizzed with happiness. 'She came knocking on my door one day and I invited her in. She was as good as she was beautiful. She even forgave me when I doubted her and loves me as much as I love her.'

'Lovely story, but kiss me.'

And he did.

This Large Print Book, for people
who cannot read normal print,
is published under the auspices of
THE ULVERSCROFT FOUNDATION

... we hope you have enjoyed this book.
Please think for a moment about those
who have worse eyesight than you ...
and are unable to even read or enjoy
Large Print without great difficulty.

You can help them by sending a
donation, large or small, to:

**The Ulverscroft Foundation,
1, The Green, Bradgate Road,
Anstey, Leicestershire, LE7 7FU,
England.**
or request a copy of our brochure for
more details.

The Foundation will use all donations
to assist those people who are visually
impaired and need special attention
with medical research, diagnosis
and treatment.

Thank you very much for your help.

1	21	41	61	81	10.
2	22	42	62	82	102
3	23	43	63	83	103
4	24	44	64	84	104
5	25	45			